IN THE SLIPS

IN THE SLIPS

IRON HORSE
MYSTERY #3

C.J. SHANE

Published by Rope's End Publishing

ISBN paperback: 978-1-951524-29-6

ISBN e-book: 978-1-951524-28-9

Typesetting services by BOOKOW.COM

Acknowledgments

Sincere thanks go to Tucson graphic designer Lynne East-Itkin for the book cover design, and to Dawn Lewis of County Durham, England, for editorial services.

Letty Valdez Mysteries

Desert Jade 2017
Dragon's Revenge 2018
Daemon Waters 2019
Direct Evidence 2022

Cat Miranda Mysteries

Kissed 2020
Fair Play 2021
The Broken Pot 2022

Iron Horse Mysteries

Take Four #1 2023
Shadow Man #2 2023
In the Slips #3 2024
Clouds #4 2024
A Closer Look #5 2024

CONTENTS

1 Visit from the Vet

Marc Tomassone pulled himself up from his sofa, took a deep breath, and stretched his arms over his head. For most of the night, he'd tossed and turned. He hadn't fallen asleep until about four a.m., and now he was awake at seven, still tired. More than tired. He admitted to himself that he was exhausted, both physically and mentally. The jet lag from such a long flight made things even worse. He knew the physical exhaustion would go away with enough sleep. If he could sleep, that is. The mental exhaustion seemed to hang on like a dark cloud. He shook his head. He was going to have to find a way to get over all the things he'd seen during the nearly a year he'd worked as a photojournalist in war zones.

He looked over at the big dog curled up into a ball in her dog crate. The door to the crate was open, but she didn't make any effort to come out. Her eyes were open, watching him. Marc shook his head. He'd tried his best to make her feel comfortable and safe with him, but nothing seemed to work. She trembled when he came near.

Marc sighed. What the hell was I thinking? he asked himself. Bringing a dog home all the way from North Africa by way of Spain? Totally nuts. He headed for the kitchen, and he made a big pot of black coffee. Strong black coffee. He looked back at the dog while he sipped the coffee. She was a big dog, a greyhound, mostly white with large rust-brown patches on her back. When he put her on the airplane, he'd learned that she weighed sixty pounds. She had big beautiful brown eyes, even when they were full of fear.

"I'm going to give you a name, and I'm going to teach you how to navigate the stairs."

The dog blinked.

Marc's apartment was on the second floor of a Spanish Revival-style home nearly one hundred years old. Some fifty years earlier, it had been remodeled and transformed into an apartment building with seven units, and then it was given the name Casa Pacifica Apartments. Casa Pacifica was located in the Iron Horse neighborhood of Tucson. Going up and down either the front or back staircase was required to get to his apartment. But the dog apparently didn't know how to climb stairs. Marc had discovered that when he had arrived home late last night. She'd stood at the bottom of the stairs, trembled, and pulled against the leash when he tried to lead her up the stairs. He'd already brought her crate in, leaving her in the car for a few minutes. Now it was her turn. There they were at the bottom of the stairs, and she wouldn't go up. So Marc carried her up. The dog went directly to her crate and curled into a ball.

Now it was early morning and a new day.

"You probably need to go out, don't you?" Marc said to the dog. He approached the crate, slipped a light-weight leash around her neck and gently pulled her out of the crate. The dog followed along with Marc as he left the apartment and walked to the stairs leading down to the first floor. But when they arrived at the stairs, immediately the dog began pulling against the leash. She refused to go down the stairs.

"Oh, good grief. You've never seen stairs before? So no up? And no down? Okay. Okay." Marc picked up the trembling dog, carried her down the stairs, and took her out into the fenced backyard of the apartment building. The dog did her thing, peeing and pooping. Then she retreated to the fenced corner, sat down, and watched him with worry in her eyes. Marc had to go pick her up again and carry her back upstairs where she went immediately into her crate. She never stopped trembling.

"I guess you've seen things and experienced things that were probably on a par with what I've seen and experienced the past year or so. I think you're traumatized. Me, too. But I'm going to make things better for both of us. I'm on a path now to live a quiet life, and I'm going to give you a quiet life, too." The dog put her head down on her front paws. She kept her eyes on him.

Marc sighed. It was good to be home. He'd grown up in Tucson, and he felt safe here. He felt safe in his apartment, too. So it's late April now, he said to himself, and it's going to be getting hot again soon. That's okay. He was back in his apartment, in his neighborhood, and among friends again. Yes, he felt safe here.

In the kitchen, Marc found an old metal pan and filled it with water. He had a small pouch of dog kibble and put that out on a paper plate. He put the water and dog food on the kitchen's tile floor. "You can have a drink and something to eat without me watching you," he said to the dog. Marc looked the other way. The dog didn't move.

"Okay. I get it. I'm going to go see Logan now. You can eat in secret."

Marc went downstairs to Logan Reid's apartment and knocked on the door. Logan, the Casa Pacifica apartment manager, opened the door almost immediately.

3

"Hey! Marc! You're home!" Logan reached out and gave Marc a quick hug.

"Yes, I came in late last night. Didn't want to wake you."

"Daddy! I can't find my backpack," Logan's five-year-old son, Charlie, called out from his bedroom.

Logan turned and said, "You left it in the bathroom. Hurry up or you'll be late to school." He turned back to Marc. "Kindergarten calls. I'll be gone most of the day doing university stuff. I'm sorry about that because I'd like to catch up with you."

"No problem. I'm not going anywhere so there's no hurry. We can catch up later."

"Sure. Did you bring that dog?"

"Yeah, you can meet her later."

"Charlie is very interested in meeting her. He likes dogs."

Just at that moment, Charlie appeared.

"Looks who's here. It's Marc," Logan said to his son.

Charlie looked at Marc and frowned. "I remember you. Sort of."

Marc grinned. "I've been gone a long time, but I bet you will remember me eventually. And you! You look like you've grown about foot!"

Charlie giggled. "Not that much." He stood up straighter.

"Come on, Charlie. Let's go." Logan turned to Marc. "I'll check in with you later. I'm glad you made it home safely."

"Me, too. Talk to you later."

Marc went back to his apartment. He found some more ground coffee beans at the back of his mostly-empty kitchen shelves, brewed another pot, and when the coffee had cooled, he added some milk and ice from the freezer.

Nice. The rest of the coffee went into a big glass jar, and that jar went into the fridge. He looked over at the water bowl. Half the water was gone, and the dog kibble had disappeared. He chuckled.

It was good to see Logan and Charlie again. Marc had always liked Logan and how he handled his job managing the apartment building. Over time, Logan had become the friend that all the other tenants looked to for information, fair play, safety, and for camaraderie, too. Living here was really a homecoming for Marc, not just to be back in his apartment, but for the friends he'd made over time at Casa Pacifica.

He sat back on the sofa and sipped the coffee. He knew he should probably take the dog to see a veterinarian. In order to be allowed into the U.S., the dog had already been vaccinated and micro-chipped. Marc wanted to register himself locally as her owner, and have her general health checked out. Yeah, she needed to be seen by a vet. Marc moved over to a small desk, opened his laptop and began searching for veterinarians. Much to his surprise, he found a mobile vet who would come to his apartment. That seemed to be a good solution. The vet would come here, and the dog wouldn't have to experience the trauma of being in a vet's office around a lot of people and other animals. So he called and made an appointment. The receptionist said that the veterinarian, Dr. Brooks, would arrive between five and six p.m.

Marc thought about the life he'd been living. To start, he was never again going to work as a photojournalist in war zones. Yes, he wanted a new, calm, peaceful life away from the violence, away from the sound of gunshots and bombs going off, away from the sounds of children screaming. Blood everywhere. Yeah, he was going to change everything. He was ready for a peaceful life. With friends. Maybe a girlfriend. And a dog. A home. He would focus on the kind of life he was going to build for himself. First, he would do his best to improve his health. Eat well. Exercise every day. He thought about getting up early and having a run every morning. It would be especially pleasurable if he could get this dog to run with him. That's what greyhounds are known for. Running. Yeah, that's what they do. Run. He looked over at the dog. She didn't move.

"One of these days, you're going to get used to me. Eventually, you are going to decide that you like me. You'll wag your tail when you see me coming. Just you wait and see."

The worried look on her face remained the same. Marc knew that she wasn't accustomed to being spoken to. Yelled at, maybe. But not spoken to in a friendly manner. "Yes, you're going to like me one of these days. I promise." The dog blinked.

Marc went to the bathroom and stared at himself in the mirror. His dark hair was longer than usual, now a mass of soft curls that almost touched his shoulders. He needed a haircut. And a shave. He'd grown a beard when he was in the field working, shaved it off before leaving for the U.S., and now it was growing back, a shadow on his jaws and chin. Hair length and beard he could fix. But what could he do about the dark shadows under his eyes? That might take some time.

"I'll get there," he spoke out loud. "I'll make a good life for myself. And I'll make a good life for that dog. Damn it." He went back to the sofa, stretched out, and fell asleep again.

The sun was moving down in the western sky when Marc woke again. He reached for his cell phone. Nearly six p.m. The sun would go down in about forty-five minutes. He heard a soft knock on his door. Maybe that's the vet. He pulled himself up and went to the door.

When he opened it, he took a step back in surprise. Standing there was one of the most beautiful women he'd ever seen. She was African American, slender and tall, maybe five feet ten inches, with very short Afro-style hair. She was dressed casually in khaki pants and a dark knit shirt. Large gold loop earrings hung from her ears, and a colorful beaded necklace was around her neck. Marc had a sudden urge to get his camera. She was seriously beautiful.

He realized he hadn't said anything. "Uh...can I help you?"

By this time, the woman had reached into her bag and retrieved a pin-on name tag. She attached it to her vest pocket. It read, 'Angela Brooks, D.V.M.'

Marc shook his head. "Gosh. I'm sorry. You're the vet. You just surprised me."

"Yes, I'm the veterinarian you requested. I came in my mobile unit, and you're my last call of the day." She looked vaguely annoyed.

"Oh, duh! I'm so sorry. I just woke up, I'm still jet lagged, and I'm sort of a mess. Please come in, Dr. Brooks." He stepped back and opened the door wide.

A look of sympathy replaced the annoyance. "Traveling from afar? Jet lag is tough. I know that from personal experience." Her eyes surveyed his living room and landed immediately on the dog curled up in the crate.

"Yeah, I just flew in late yesterday from Spain. Before that I was in Casablanca. That's in Morocco. And before that, Sudan and Yemen. And northern Nigeria. And Ukraine."

The veterinarian's eyebrows went up. "Whoa. I bet you have some stories to tell, Mr. Tomassone. What were you doing in all those countries?"

"Photojournalism. I was taking photos of the conflicts."

Angela nodded. She approached the crate and knelt down. "What's this beauty's name?"

"I don't know. And you can call me me Marc. That will be easier."

"Okay, Marc." She looked up at him, a question on her face. "What about the dog? You don't know her name?"

Marc winced. "She's one of my stories, Dr. Brooks. No, I don't know her name."

"We need to come up with a good name for her and use it so she'll get used to it. Has she shown any signs of aggression?"

"No," Marc said. "Actually, she seems terrified of everything. I think maybe she's spent much of her life in a crate or a cage or some kind of enclosure."

Dr. Brooks nodded. She reached out slowly with one hand and extended her fingers toward the dog's nose. The dog's nose touched her fingers, sniffed, then pulled back. Her worried gaze went from Dr. Brooks to Marc and back to the veterinarian again.

Dr. Brooks reached into her bag and pulled out a small dog biscuit. "Here you go, sweetheart," she said in a soft voice.

The dog took the dog biscuit and began crunching it.

"That's a good sign. With a treat now and then, we can convince her that we're friendly." Dr. Brooks stood up. "How do you get her to come out of the cage?"

"She doesn't have a collar so I put this leash around her neck," he gestured behind him, "and I sort of pull her out. She'll come out with a little nudging."

"That's called a slip leash. So she accepts that?"

"Yeah. She comes out then she just stands there and trembles. I have to carry her downstairs so she can go out and do her business. She doesn't know how to go up and down stairs."

"That can't be easy on you. I bet she weighs at least sixty pounds."

"Yeah. That's exactly how much she weighs. But I don't have any other option. She's too scared to navigate the stairs."

"That's sad. Please bring her out now so I can take a look at her."

Marc leashed the dog and urged her to come out. She crept out and stood there trembling.

Dr. Brooks began a slow and careful examination of the dog. She ran her hands over the dog's body, palpitated her abdomen, looked into the dog's eyes, ears and mouth, and checked her gums, too. Then the doctor pulled a stethoscope from her bag and listened to the dog's lungs and stomach. She inserted a thermometer into the dog's anus to take her temperature. Then the doctor's hands returned to the dog, stroking her while examining her joints and spine. She hesitated when she came in contact with the dog's lower right-front leg. All the time the veterinarian's hands were on the dog, Dr. Brooks spoke softly in a low voice to the dog. Marc was surprised that the dog accepted all this so easily. The vet clearly knew what she was doing.

Dr Brooks turned to Marc and asked, "You have vaccination papers, right? Dogs have to be vaccinated before they can enter the U.S."

"Yes. I have her papers. She's been micro-chipped, too."

"How did you come to meet this beauty?"

"I was heading home, and I stopped by to see a friend in Morocco. We went to the dog races. His idea. I'm not into that kind of thing normally, but he wanted to go." Marc stood up. "Turns out that for a while now, my friend has been rescuing some of these dogs from the racetrack and finding them new homes. Somehow he convinced me to adopt her. I know it's crazy." He shook his head.

The veterinarian smiled. "I bet those big brown eyes were hard to resist."

"I guess. I don't know what I was thinking. Or not thinking." Marc frowned.

"You mentioned Spain."

"Apparently my friend has found homes for several of these racing greyhounds, but he takes them to Spain first because it's easier to ship them to other European countries and to the U.S. from there. He bought this dog from the race track people, shipped her to Spain, and I met him again there in Madrid. I had to get the dog registered and vaccinated and micro-chipped to fly her to America and get her through customs and all that." He went to his briefcase and pulled out papers. He handed them to Dr. Brooks.

"I see the Spanish documents. But what about these? The text is all in French or Arabic," she said.

"Yes, these are the papers from the original owner in Morocco. I don't know either language. I guess I should get this translated into English."

"I speak and read French. This says 'Nom: Saint Guinefort.' So her name is Saint Guinefort. That's a mouthful. How about if we call her Guine for short. We could change the spelling to Gwen so people will know how to say it. Or just tell them to say 'Gwen.' Or 'Gwenny'? How about that? Gwenny? What do you think? And you can call me Angela." She smiled.

"Okay. Change her name to 'Gwenny'. Sounds good to me." Marc looked at the dog and said, "Hey, Gwenny. Dr. Brooks...uh...I mean Angela...just gave you a name. And you are standing there and accepting her examination. I bet you like her touching you like that."

While the veterinarian gently ran her hands over Gwenny's sleek body, Marc started searching on his cell phone. "Hey, Wikipedia says Saint Guinefort was a greyhound in France in the thirteenth century. The local folk thought of her as a folk saint."

"That's interesting," the doctor said.

"Gwenny, are you a saint?" Marc chuckled.

Gwenny raised her head and looked at him. She looked a tiny bit relaxed. Angela the Vet was already helping the dog with her soft strokes and soft voice.

Angela pulled out a hand scanner to check for a microchip. "Yes, Gwenny has a microchip. I'm going to register her with Pima County so you'll be on record as her owner. I need your contact information. You'll get a tag in the mail to put on her collar. You need to get a collar." She handed her cell phone to Marc, and he filled in the required information.

"So with the microchip, if she runs off, it will be easier to return her to me, right?" Marc shook his head. He wondered if Gwenny might be waiting for a chance to run away. Probably not. That would be too scary for her.

"Yes. But you need to keep her safe. No running off. She might get hit by a car." Angela sat back on the floor and looked at Marc.

"Let's sit on the sofa," Marc suggested. They moved to the sofa, and Gwenny went back to her crate.

"Here's what I've learned from this preliminary exam. Gwenny is about four years old. Her front right leg was broken at some point. I can feel where the bone broke and healed, although I would like to get an x-ray to know how bad the break was. There's evidence, too, that she's been bred."

"She's had puppies?"

"Yes, I'm pretty sure about that. Likely more than one litter."

"But I thought she was a racing dog."

"She probably was at some point," Angela said, "but her race track days may have ended when she broke her leg. If she was fast, they probably decided to breed her with a fast male and produce fast puppies."

Marc frowned. "One of the men I talked to at the track told me that the racing hounds were taken out every day for exercise. I'm wondering now if Gwenny's leg and her pregnancies meant she was stuck in a cage most of the time."

"Very likely. Her muscles are a bit on the flaccid side."

"So she's about four years old? What is that in dog years? One dog year equals seven human years, right? So four times seven is twenty-eight?"

Angela shook her head. "That's not really accurate. The size of the dog makes a big difference. Gwenny is a greyhound so she's a big girl. I'd say four years is more like forty-five in human years.

"Wow. So she's entering middle age?"

"That's right."

"I hope I can give her a better life," Marc said.

"You already are giving her a better life."

Marc felt this wave of….of what?...relief?...come over him. Maybe that's why he'd adopted her. To help her and himself get over a lot of sadness and to make a better life for them both.

"So have you been sitting here in this room and just sort of hanging out with Gwenny?"

"Yes. I'm on the sofa. She's in the crate. I don't bother her unless it's time to go outside."

"That's probably the very best thing. She's becoming accustomed to you. She knows by now that you're unlikely to hit her or yell at her."

Marc shook his head. "No way would I do that. I want her to trust me."

Angela Brooks smiled. "Look. I wonder if we could try something. I have a special interest in what's called veterinary behavioral health. It's a specialty in helping animals get over trauma and then begin to lead a more normal life. Sometimes this means dealing with aggression, but in this case, it's just the opposite. She's obviously very timid and afraid. Would you be willing for me to come by here in my off hours and work with Gwenny a little? I think I could help her get over her trauma. No charge. It would be a favor to me, actually, because I'm trying to learn more about animal behavior therapy."

Marc grinned. "Gosh, that would be great. Tomorrow? Or Sunday?"

Angela smiled. "I can't tomorrow because I'm working. But how about Sunday afternoon? That would be good for me. How about if I come around three?"

"We'll be here."

Angela stood up. "I'll see you then." She collected her equipment, turned to Gwenny and said, "Goodbye, sweetie. I'll see you Sunday." The dog's ears went up. Angela turned to Marc and said, "By the way, what does that sign on the street mean? It says 'Iron Horse District.'"

"This part of town is where the railroad executives and workers lived when the railroad first came to Tucson. That was about a hundred years ago."

"Oh, I see. The Iron Horse refers to the railroad."

"Yes, you got it." Marc followed her to the door.

Angela turned and smiled. She stuck out her hand. Marc took it. "Nice to meet you, Mr. Marc Tomassone."

Marc grinned. "My pleasure, Dr. Angela Brooks."

She turned and left, heading toward the front downward staircase.

Marc closed the door behind her, still grinning. He felt much better than he had earlier in the day. What a lovely woman. He returned to his place on the sofa and began thinking about getting something to eat for supper. Maybe Gwenny would go with him for a short walk around the neighborhood.

Suddenly Marc heard voices screaming and yelling. The sounds were coming from the front of the Casa Pacifica building. He looked over at Gwenny. Her ears were up again. She'd heard the noise, too. Marc jumped up and headed out the door, closing it behind him.

2 An Uninvited Visitor

Marc sprinted down the hallway and took the stairs down to the ground floor two steps at a time. Logan was coming out of his apartment door, and Marc heard him say, "Charlie, you stay here with Zoey." Logan closed the door behind him. Someone was coming down the stairs behind Marc. He turned and saw Li, another resident that Marc had known before he left Tucson. Logan and Li followed Marc out to the front of the Casa Pacifica apartments.

The yelling and screaming had stopped.

Standing on the sidewalk was Angela Brooks, the veterinarian. Next to her was a woman that Marc had never seen before. The two women were holding hands and staring at Angela's mini-van. Although the sun was low in the sky to the west, there was still enough light for Marc to see a sign on the side of the van. It said, "Tucson Mobile Veterinary Services." There was a graphic of a dog and a cat grinning at them.

Li was standing next to Marc now. "Hey, Marc. Welcome home."

"Hey. I just got back."

"What's going on here?" Logan said in a firm voice.

Marc took a few steps forward toward Angela. "Are you okay?"

Angela turned to him. "Yeah. Just a little shook up." She released the other woman's hand. "She helped me."

"What happened?" Logan asked. He turned to the other woman and said, "And who are you?"

"Xochi Navarro. I'm here to see an apartment that will be available soon. This *chica* was coming out to her van, and we both saw this *pendejo* slashing her tires with some kind of big knife."

"I tried to stop him. I ran up to him and shoved him. He just turned toward me and hit me," Angela added. She touched her cheek.

"Oh, no!" Marc said. "Your face. He hit you in the face?" He felt a rush of anger come over him. He was annoyed with himself that he hadn't been there to stop this assault on her.

Angela nodded. "And he hit her, too." She turned to the other woman. "What did you say your name is?"

"Xochi." She turned to the three men. "She's right. When I came running to help her, he punched me here." She patted her chin. "Yeah, in the face. Just like her." Her long, dark hair was in disarray, and the look on her face could best be described as furious. She looked back at Angela. "What's your name?"

"Angela Brooks."

"She's my veterinarian," Marc said. "I'm Marc."

"Okay," Logan said. "We need to call the cops. You'll both have to report this as an assault as well as vandalism. Dr. Brooks, you can show the cops what that guy did to your van."

"And you are?" Angela asked Logan.

"Sorry. I'm Logan Reid, manager of the Casa Pacifica apartments. And this is Li. He lives here, too. Give me a minute." He turned, took a few steps away and made the call to the Tucson Police Department.

Angela walked around her mini-van, peering at the tires. "That bastard slashed all four of the tires." She shook her head in irritation. "I guess I'll have to call a taxi to get home, and deal with this tomorrow because it looks like the van will have to be towed. Our vet clinic has a technician who can get new tires and put them on the van."

"I'll take you home," Marc said.

"Did he break into your van? Was anything taken from the interior?" Logan asked. He was at her side now.

"No." Angela was looking into the windows now. "Looks like he didn't have time to break in."

"Okay. The cops are coming. We'll let them handle this." He turned to Xochi Navarro. "And you, Ms. Navarro. I received your text this afternoon so I was expecting you. Do you want to see the apartment while we wait for the cops?"

"Yes, please. You can call me Xochi. That's a Mexican name, short for Xochitl. Xochi is spelled with an 'x' but sounds like SO-chee."

Li was watching Xochi with a smile on his face. He inserted himself in the conversation now. "You can call me Li. That's a Chinese name, short for Liang. Spelled 'Li' but sounds like Lee."

"That's easy," Xochi said. She nodded and returned his smile.

"You'll be seeing more of me because I'll be working with Marc's dog," Angela said to Logan.

"Fine. I'm Logan. So we're all on a first name basis. Angela, I'm sorry about this. We don't usually have people being assaulted or acts of vandalism like this in our neighborhood." Well, not exactly true, Logan said to himself, but this wasn't the time to go into details of what he considered some very abnormal events that had occurred fairly recently. Yes, normally the Iron Horse neighborhood was pretty quiet.

"That's good to know," Xochi said.

Logan turned to Marc. "So you'll take Angela home?"

"Yes, if that's okay with you, Angela?"

"That would be very helpful. I don't live far from here."

Much to everyone's surprise, a Tucson police car pulled up to the curb at that very moment. Two uniformed cops stepped out of their vehicle. One uniformed cop stayed with the patrol car as the other man approached the group.

Logan stepped forward. "I'm Logan Reid, the apartment manager here. I'm the one who called you." He gestured first to Angela. "This is Dr. Angela Brooks, and the van is hers. This is one of our regular tenants who just returned from a trip, Marc Tomassone. David Liang is also a resident here. We call him Li. Dr. Brooks was visiting Marc about his dog." He nodded to Xochi. "And this is Xochi Navarro who is here to take a look at an apartment that is coming open soon. Dr. Brooks and Ms. Navarro were both assaulted, and Dr. Brooks's van was vandalized." Logan noticed the policeman's name on his uniform, "Cooper."

"Did any of you see the perpetrator? Could you identify him if you saw him again?" Officer Cooper asked.

"Marc, Li, and I came out here when we heard them yelling. We didn't see him. I guess it was a him. I don't know."

"How about you two?"

"I'm pretty sure he was a man. He was dressed in black with a black hoodie, and he had on a mask. I couldn't see his face," Angela said.

"Yeah, he was maybe five feet ten or so, not heavy but not thin. His face was in the shadows, and yeah, he had on a mask, too." Xochi looked at Angela.

"Yes, that's right. The mask was a dark color, too," she responded.

"Okay, ladies," the policeman said. "Please step aside here. I have a few more questions for you. You guys can go if you want." He turned and nodded to the other cop.

The two women followed Officer Cooper a few feet away while he pulled a notepad from his pocket. He began asking them both questions in a low voice.

Logan turned to Marc. "What do you know about this?"

"Not much," Marc shrugged. "Dr. Brooks, Angela, provides a mobile veterinary service. I mean she has this van, and she goes out on calls to people who need a veterinarian. I think she's in the vet's office sometimes, too. She came this afternoon to check out my dog, and she's coming back on Sunday."

"You have a dog?" Li asked. "That's cool."

"Yeah, also it's kind of crazy. She's a female greyhound. I got her from a race track in Morocco."

"Wow. That's a long way away. And a big dog. What's her name?" Li asked.

"Gwenny. She's kind of traumatized. She shakes and trembles all the time like she's scared of everything, especially people. Dr. Brooks is going to try to help her."

"I guess coming from North Africa all the way to Arizona would be kind of traumatic. As for me, I sort of share a cat with Frida now. The cat's name is Bonita, and I take care of her sometimes. Actually, I take care of her a lot. She stays indoors most of the time so the coyotes won't get her."

"How's Frida doing?" Marc asked. "I look forward to seeing her again."

"She's great. Causing trouble as usual. She's leading a strike now for some restaurant workers."

Marc nodded and smiled. "That sounds just like Frida."

"My son Charlie loves animals," Logan said. "I'm sure he'd like to meet Gwenny. And you'll want to meet Zoey, too. She's new here. Not super new. She moved into the apartment downstairs a few months ago. I'm talking about the apartment that those two losers used to rent. They caused so much trouble and damage to the place that I had to evict them. Zoey and I are…" he hesitated.

Li laughed. "Logan and Zoey are totally hot for each other."

Logan couldn't help himself. His face was warm now, but he laughed, too. "Let's just say we're getting to know each other. Really well. Charlie's crazy about her."

Marc grinned and nodded. "I'd like to get to know Dr. Brooks. Really well. She's really nice. And kind."

"And beautiful?" Li grinned.

"Yeah, that, too," Marc laughed. "And now, after this happening, I want to make sure she stays safe."

Logan noticed that the cop who was not interviewing Angela and Xochi was taking photos of the damage done to the van's tires. It was dusky enough now that his phone camera flashed a light with every photo.

Officer Cooper folded his notebook to close it, and he turned back to Logan. "You don't happen to have security cameras on this property, do you?"

"No," Logan answered. "Maybe it's time to get one, or more than one."

The police officer looked at Angela and Xochi. "Okay, I have your statements now. We may get back to you, and Miss Navarro and Dr. Brooks, too, with more questions. We'll be looking for a suspect."

The two cops departed. Logan turned to Xochi. "Come with me, and I'll show you the apartment up-stairs. I need to stop first to let my son and Zoey know we're all okay. Marc, let's get together tomorrow and catch up."

Marc nodded. "Sure." He turned to Angela. "Here. Let me take your bag. My car is in the back of the apartment building in the alley parking lot."

"Thanks, Marc." Angela followed him.

* * *

Logan popped his head into his apartment and grabbed his briefcase. "Zoey, I'm showing Nina's old apartment to a possible new tenant. It won't take long." Zoey waved and smiled. He turned and led Xochi upstairs. "The apartment that is coming open is right above my apartment. You realize this is a two-bedroom apartment, right?"

"Yes, I know about the two bedrooms. I'm friends with Nina, and she told me all about the apartment. She said some guy was staying here temporarily."

"Yeah. Cass Cosay. He and one of our tenants downstairs, Dylan Scott, ended up getting involved with each other. Actually they've already moved north to live together on the Ft. Apache reservation. They plan to get married sometime, this fall maybe. So it's been kind of like musical chairs with the apartments around here recently. But what about a roommate, boyfriend, husband, whatever?"

"No, just me. I need the extra room. I'll explain in a minute."

Logan unlocked the apartment door and stepped aside so that Xochi could enter first.

"I usually try to get references from future tenants," he said. "But Nina spoke well of you."

"And she spoke well of you, Logan Reid." She grinned at him.

"Nina has been helpful with her recommendations."

"That's a big reason why I'm here. Nina said you are a good guy, and you can be trusted. She actually said you are like everyone's big brother."

"Oh, gosh. That sounds like Nina," Logan said. "I'm not anyone's big brother. I just try to be helpful and fair."

Xochi looked around the open living space, walked into the kitchen and opened a couple of cabinets, then headed to the two bedrooms. One had a large double bed, a chest, and a small table with a lamp at the bedside. The other bedroom was full of cardboard boxes. She looked in closets, then headed for the bathroom. When she came out, she approached Logan and said, "This looks perfect for me."

"So what about needing two bedrooms? If you don't have a roommate, what's the extra bedroom for?"

"I'm an artist. I need the extra room to do my artwork, and sometimes I teach small classes. That means I'll have four or even five students who will be here for a few hours. I'll let you know when I'm having a class."

Logan frowned. "I'm concerned about the effect of painting, or whatever you're doing, on the carpet in that room. Art can be kind of messy."

"I'm not a painter. I'm a book artist. I make artist's books."

A look of bewilderment came over Logan's face. "Artist's books? You mean like those old antique books, the ones with the beautiful covers? You can make those?"

"Yes, I can, but that's not what I do. An artist's book is a work of art. Instead of paint on canvas, the art comes in the form of a book. Let me find a definition for you." She opened her cell phone and clicked on a couple of links. "Here's what the Smithsonian says. 'An artist's book is a medium of artistic expression that uses the form or function of "book" as inspiration.' And Wikipedia says that artist's books 'are works of art that utilize the form of the book. They are often published in small editions, though they are sometimes produced as one-of-a-kind objects.'" She stuck her phone back in her pocket and smiled at Logan.

Logan grinned. "I love books. And I would very much like to see an artist's book."

"Sure! I have multiple examples of my own books, and also books that I've collected from other book artists."

"So, no messy paint or clay or glass and metal in the carpet."

"Nope. Maybe some thread or torn paper. If my students and I do anything messy, like paint some paste paper, we'll do it outside."

"Yes, I definitely would like to see some artist's books. And I don't know what paste paper is."

"I'll send you some links so you can look at collections on the web. There's a lot of images of artist's books on the web. After I move in, I'll show you some real books, and some paste paper, too. Maybe you'll want to take my class someday." She grinned.

"Maybe. Okay. I'll get the leash." He reached for his briefcase and pulled out two copies of the lease. "When you sign the lease, you are agreeing to pay your rent on the first of the month, you agree not to do damage to the property, and you have to behave. You and your fellow artists can't be having any wild parties. And if you get a pet, you have to let me know."

Xochi chuckled. "That's not going to happen. I'm really a quiet person because I focus on my art. And my students are quiet, too. So no wild parties. As far as pets are concerned, I've been thinking about that. I'll let you know. Do I have to report goldfish?"

Logan grinned. "No. I was thinking of a dog or a cat. And I need rental deposit, too. Do you agree to all that?"

"Yes. Where do I sign?"

Logan put the lease copies on the table, handed Xochi a pen and said, "Sign both copies. One for me and one for you. When were you planning on moving in? I ask because the previous tenants haven't retrieved all their stuff yet. That's what all those boxes are in the second bedroom. That should happen soon."

"How about the first of the month? I've paid my rent on my current apartment until then. Also I need some time to pack up my possessions and my art supplies. I have a lot of different kinds of paper. Is there any way to get all the furniture out of the room with the boxes? I don't need an extra bed."

"Yes, I can arrange that. And about the boxes. I should mention that Cass and Dylan are coming back here this weekend to move the rest of her stuff out of her old apartment, and haul it back to the rez. Cass told me that he's coming in a pickup truck for that. Some of the boxes in that bedroom are Nina's. Dylan and Cass will also be moving the rest of Nina's boxes downstairs into Dylan's old apartment. That will clear up the space for you."

"I see what you mean about musical chairs."

As they left the apartment and headed downstairs, Logan added, "Oh, I want to mention that we have a Sunday potluck dinner every week. You're invited to that, too. You can come this Sunday if you want and meet everyone."

"Thanks. Nina told me about that, too. Maybe I'll make an edible artist's book for the potluck."

Logan laughed. "I'd love to see that. My son Charlie would find that very entertaining, especially if ice cream is involved."

Xochi waved goodbye, and Logan returned to his apartment. He sat down next to Zoey on the sofa. Charlie was on her lap, leaning up against her. He was falling asleep.

Logan's phone beeped. He looked at the incoming message, clicked on a couple of links, and said. "Wow!"

"What is it?"

"Artist's books. Amazing." He looked at Zoey and smiled. "I could show you, but you have to kiss me first."

Zoey laughed. "That's a high price to pay."

"You'll see some really amazing art." He wiggled his eyebrows.

"Okay. You've convinced me." She leaned toward him and kissed him.

Her movement woke Charlie. "Daddy, I'm hungry."

"Okay. I'll make us something to eat."

* * *

"So where do you live?" Marc asked Angela.

"Not too far. I'm in the Rincon Heights neighborhood just a few blocks to the east."

"My car is parked in the back. Do you have an apartment in that part of town?"

"Not exactly. It's a small house in an older neighborhood of mostly small houses. I'm house sitting. I'm friends with the person who lives there, and when I moved here, she asked me to stay at her house while she was gone. She's coming back soon. I'll be looking for a new place then."

Marc nodded. "So you haven't been in Tucson very long?"

"No, about two months. I like it here. I'm house sitting for a woman I met when I was participating in a volunteer vet program. Her name is Cynthia, and she's a veterinary assistant. When I was in my last year of vet school, I participated as a volunteer to provide vet services on Native American reservations. We stayed in Arizona the longest time, and I visited Tucson then."

"Yeah, we have twenty-two federally recognized tribes. I guess you went to the Navajo rez and the O'odham rez near Tucson?"

"Yes, and the Hopi and two Apache reservations and a couple of smaller ones."

"Did they accept you and treat you well? I mean, there's not a lot of black people on the rez."

"They treated me very well. The kids were adorable. They followed me everywhere, mostly little girls. They were giggling the entire time." She laughed. "I think I was quite the novelty."

"You set a good example. Now those little girls know they can grow up to study science, be a doctor or a veterinarian, and they don't have to be white."

"Yes, that's true. I did think about that. I guess I'm an example of what's possible."

"Where did you come from originally?"

"Arabi. St. Bernard Parish. That's part of the New Orleans metro area."

"Ah. So that explains that." He chuckled.

"What?"

"Sometimes when you talk, you sort of…" He hesitated.

"I sound like a Southern gal?"

"Yes, so very charming."

"Oh, good. So you don't think I'm a hick."

Marc looked at her and said in a serious tone. "Of course not. It's obvious that you are brilliant."

Now it was Angela's turn to laugh. "You're funny." She paused and then said, "Marc, I have an idea."

"Okay. What's your idea?"

"Let's take Gwenny with us." She looked at Marc and smiled.

"You don't think she'll freak out?"

"I think she'll go along for a little outing with us because she has to. She'll be scared at first. But she'll begin to realize that she's safe with us. Then you can come back to your place and feed her supper. She'll associate us with happy times."

Marc chuckled. "Happy times. That sounds good." He thought to himself that Gwenny wouldn't be the only one who associated Angela with happy times. He hadn't laughed this much in months. Too long.

They went through the side entrance of Casa Pacifica, through the small kitchen and laundry and up the back stairs to Marc's apartment. Gwenny was curled up in a ball in her crate. She lifted her head and looked at them when they entered the apartment.

"Where's that slip leash?" Angela asked.

Marc found the leash, quickly placed it over Gwenny's head and around her neck, and urged her out of the crate. He carried Gwenny down the stairs, and Angela took over leading Gwenny on the leash to the car. Then Marc lifted Gwenny into the back seat of his car, he and Angela got into the car, too, and off they went.

3 HOME

Angela gave Marc directions to her home, and then she turned to look at Gwenny in the backseat. The dog was curled up in a ball, but her head was up and she was looking around. When she saw Angela looking at her, she held very still and peered back.

"Hello, Gwenny," Angela said in a soft voice. "You're so beautiful, Gwenny."

"You're repeating her name so she'll learn it?" Marc asked.

"Yes, exactly. And every time she gets a caress or a treat, we'll call her by her name."

After a few moments of silence, Marc glanced over at Angela. "I'm curious about your volunteer gig here in Arizona. What kind of things did you do?"

"Regular vet stuff like give vaccinations to pets, mainly dogs and cats, and spay and neuter dogs, especially the feral dogs."

"Feral dogs?"

"Yes, it's common to have dogs go wild and produce a lot of puppies on the reservations. Sometimes they even mate with coyotes, but that's not common because of differences in the breeding cycle. These feral dogs can become aggressive when looking for food, and they can attack farm animals and even children. So spaying and neutering reduces the feral population. We gave them rabies vaccinations, too. Some of the tribal members helped us to catch the dogs."

"Interesting. I didn't know that about feral dogs. What else?"

"We provided care for farm animals like horses, sheep, cows, and hogs. I know more about the domestic pets so I focused on those, usually dogs or cats, and sometimes a pet pig. It was on my volunteer trip to the Navajo reservation that I learned more about behavior therapy for animals from one of the other vets. I knew I had to follow up on that."

"I hope you can help Gwenny. I want her to like me."

"Oh, she will. I promise you that."

They were at a red light now. Marc looked at Angela. "Thank you." He didn't know what else to say.

"Also, did you know that there's a volunteer group that provides free vet care to the pets of homeless people here in Tucson?"

Marc shook his head. "This is all new to me." He had this sudden thought about doing a feature made up of a series of photos on this project, generate interest in it, blah, blah. He wondered if he would always think like that, like a photojournalist. At other times, he didn't ever want to touch a camera again.

"Also I should mention...because you said you were in Ukraine...that I did a volunteer gig there, too," Angela said.

"Really? Oh, boy. What was that like?" Marc paused and frowned. "Was it difficult for you? I guess you heard bombs going off all the time."

"Yes. They tried to send us to areas in the country that were safer, but even so, sometimes those drones appeared and dropped explosives. Luckily, we never got hit. We had two teams. One team went to the zoos to take care of zoo animals. The other team, my team, cared for domestic animals. That meant those pets still living with their owners or in shelters. But it also meant caring for a lot of animals, mainly dogs, living on the street. Their owners had to flee the war and couldn't take the dogs with them. We provided medical care and food, and if possible, moved them into a shelter where they could get regular meals."

Marc glanced at Angela. She had tears in her eyes.

"Something sad happened, didn't it?"

"Yeah," she sighed. "Oh, there's my house." She pointed to an older bungalow-style home on the right side of the road. A big mesquite provided shade in the front yard. Four concrete steps led up to the covered porch.

Marc pulled over and parked at the curb.

"I'll tell you what happened if sometime you tell me about your experiences," she said.

Marc frowned. "Okay." He sighed. He hoped that she would forget and never ask him.

Angela looked straight ahead. "There was this very friendly dog. A collie mix, I would guess. Beautiful dog. He definitely was somebody's pet. He was coming toward us from almost a block away with his tail wagging. Suddenly, a drone zipped past and dropped something, maybe a hand grenade. It hit the dog and exploded. His entire side, from front to back, was ripped open. His guts and organs spilled out onto the ground. He howled in pain, screaming really. I ran over to him. He stopped wailing and just whimpered when he saw me. He thought I was going to help him, but I couldn't. Half his internal organs were on the ground. Intestines. Stomach." Tears began to roll down her cheeks.

"I'm sorry, Angela. I shouldn't have asked." Marc took her hand in his.

She shook her head side-to-side. "I looked around, and I saw a soldier nearby. I waved for him to come over. He took one look at the dog and shook his head. I don't speak Ukrainian. I just pointed to his gun and then to the dog's head. He nodded. I stroked the dog's head and told him that he was going over the Rainbow Bridge now and no need to be afraid. Then I stepped back, the soldier shot the dog in its head, and he put the dog out of its misery. It just took a second."

They were silent for a couple of minutes.

"War is stupid," Marc said.

Angela looked at him and nodded. "Totally stupid. So much suffering for nothing."

"I'm sorry that happened to you."

"Yeah, I'm sorry, too, but it came with the job. It's good for me to talk to a kindred spirit."

That made Marc feel better. He liked the idea of being Angela's kindred spirit.

"Time for me to go in. Thanks so much for the ride." She was smiling again.

Marc hesitated, then said, "If you don't mind, Angela. I'd like to go in with you and check things out. I realize that maybe I'm sort of paranoid because I spent so much time in war zones, but I want you to be safe. It just seems weird to me that your van was vandalized. I mean, why *your* van? There were other cars on the street that were untouched. And why all four tires? It seems too much, like maybe it was directed at you, or maybe your veterinary practice, or something. I don't really know. I just want to make sure you aren't a target. I hope you feel you can trust me, and let me into your house to look around."

Angela looked at Marc, into his eyes, for a long moment. "I trust you. Yes, please come in. And bring Gwenny."

She looked back at Gwenny. "Hey, girl. Guess what? You're going to go up four steps!"

Marc chuckled. "So you have an ulterior motive?"

"Of course. Gwenny and I are in therapy mode. Just give me a minute. I'll be right out."

Angela walked quickly to her house, unlocked the door and went in. The porch light came on. Meanwhile Marc put the slip leash on Gwenny and urged her out of the car. Just as they got to the steps that led up to the porch, Angela reappeared. She was grinning.

Gwenny stopped at the foot of the stairs. Marc attempted to lead her up, but she balked.

"Only four steps, Gwenny Girl," Marc said quietly. "You can do it."

Angela stepped forward, came down two steps, held out her hand, and said, "Smell this, Gwenny. Climb these steps, and you get a big piece of roasted chicken." Just as Gwenny reached for the chicken, Angela returned to the porch. She held the chicken out to Gwenny, but out of reach.

Gwenny whined. Angela chuckled.

Marc grinned. "She's definitely interested."

Very carefully, very slowly, with fear and trepidation, Gwenny went up the stairs one by one, one paw, one leg at a time. When she reached the top, Angela stroked her head, gave her the chicken, and told Gwenny that she was the bravest dog in the world. Marc was chuckling now.

"Gwenny, your therapist — that's me, sweetie — your therapist thinks something bad happened to you once around stairs. A fall maybe? Or maybe some jerk threw you down some stairs? You have a lot of anxiety when you encounter stairs. But those days are over. Marc is going to give you the best life ever, better than you ever imagined."

Marc nodded. Yes. For sure.

Angela stood up and looked at Marc. "Well done, Marc."

"What? I didn't do anything."

"Yes, you did. You stayed with her. You didn't push her. You let her go at her own pace. You didn't yell at her. And you said encouraging words. Perfect."

"Oh." He didn't know what to say.

"Marc and Gwenny. Please come in." Angela opened the screen door and held it open for them. Marc and Gwenny walked in. Marc looked around. Nice living room with a dining area at the far end, a small fireplace, cream-colored paint on the walls, a comfortable sofa. Very homey.

"You want to take the leash? I'll look around." Marc went room by room: kitchen, two bedrooms, the bath. He checked closets. No one there. He checked windows and the back door. All locked. He opened the back door and looked out. Although the sun had set, there was enough light to see a small fenced yard with potted plants and a garden bed with a few tomato plants. Neat and tidy. No sign of intruders anywhere.

Marc returned to the living room. Angela was sitting on the sofa. Gwenny was standing in front of her enjoying Angela's strokes and pets. "Looks good, Angela. It doesn't appear that anyone has attempted to break in. Thank you for indulging me." He reached out and stroked Gwenny, too. "I guess I'd better go home now."

She smiled and nodded. "Let's see what she does about going down the stairs."

They rose, Marc put the slip leash on again, and they headed outside. Gwenny hesitated at the top of the stairs, then she rapidly descended. Marc went with her so the leash wouldn't get too tight.

"Excellent," Angela said. She reached into her pocket and pulled out a big dog biscuit. She went down the stairs to Gwenny and gave her the dog biscuit. Gwenny began crunching it immediately. Angela looked at Marc. "This was fun. Let's do it again. And I'll see you Sunday afternoon." She leaned forward and kissed him on the cheek.

Marc grinned all the way home.

Back at Casa Pacifica again, Marc and Gwenny went to the foot of the stairs leading to his apartment. Again, she hesitated. "Oh, Gwenny, just you wait. Angela is coming on Sunday, and I bet she brings some chicken with her. You'll be going up and down those stairs in a flash." He picked the dog up and carried her to his apartment. She went immediately to her crate.

"Okay, Gwenny. It's time to eat supper." Gwenny raised her head at the sound of his voice. Marc filled her water bowl and put some kibble in an old salad bowl he'd found in the kitchen cabinet. He made himself a sandwich. That meant thawing out some bread he found in the freezer and opening a can of tuna. He sat on the sofa, ate the sandwich, and drank a warm beer from a six-pack that he found in a lower cabinet shelf. He really needed to go buy some food at the market. Instead, he turned on the TV and ignored Gwenny.

After a while, Gwenny came out of her crate, walked quickly past him to her food bowl, and she began eating her kibble. Marc grinned, but said nothing. He pretended he hadn't even seen her. He went back to watching the TV. There was some show on about antiques. He liked the show even though he knew nothing about antiques. He liked it because there were no bombs going off, and no one was carrying a gun. He began to feel relaxed, and he continued to ignore Gwenny. Eventually the dog finished her supper and returned to her crate.

After another hour of television antiques, Marc carried Gwenny down the stairs again, and they went together on a walk around the Iron Horse neighborhood. Everything in the neighborhood was quiet, although he could hear the sound of traffic on the multi-lane parkway to the south. Occasionally the sounds of music drifted from the clubs on Fourth Avenue to the west. But everything was quiet enough that Gwenny never became alarmed. She never pulled on the leash, nor did she resist moving forward. The walk was good for them both.

Marc decided to go to bed early so he could return to a regular schedule. Get back on Tucson time. Be a Tucsonan again. Do Tucson things. Eat tacos. Go to basketball and football games. Eat more tacos. Hang out with friends. Eat burritos. Take Gwenny on long walks. Maybe take her to the Rillito River for a run in the sandy riverbed. Forget about the horrors he'd seen. Start a new life.

He thought about Angela. He looked forward to Sunday afternoon when she would return.

* * *

On Saturday morning, Marc woke up just after the sun rose. When he opened his eyes, he could see Gwenny standing at the door. She looked at him.

"You need to go out, don't you?" He didn't bother getting dressed. Wearing his t-shirt and boxer shorts, he picked her up and took her outside where she did her thing. He sat on the back porch and enjoyed the morning sun. Then it was time to go back upstairs. He left food in the dog bowl for Gwenny's breakfast, and he ate a quick breakfast. He took a shower and shaved off that scruff on his face. He'd deal with his too-long hair later. When he came out, Gwenny had finished her breakfast.

Marc heard a noise downstairs, kind of a loud motor vehicle kind of noise, so he went to check it out. There was a big tow truck with a noisy engine pulling Angela's veterinary service van up onto the trailer. Logan was there talking to a man Marc had never seen. Marc approached them.

Logan turned to Marc, nodded, and said to the man, "This is Eric Carlson. He works for the veterinary clinic. He brought the tow truck guy here to haul the van away."

Marc nodded to the guy standing near Logan. He noticed that the man was about thirty years old, and dressed in jeans and a dark blue sweat shirt. He had dark blond hair and a scruffy beard. He didn't smile when he returned the nod.

The man turned back to Logan and said, "Okay. We're done here. The tow truck driver will give me a ride."

"Good. Thanks," said Logan. The man walked to the tow truck and got into the passenger side. Logan turned to Marc. "Everything going okay?"

"Yep. I'm feeding Gwenny now. Would it be okay to bring her to your apartment? I'd like to talk to you about something, and I'd like for Charlie to meet Gwenny."

"Sure. Come now if you want. Let's just make sure Charlie stays safe. I don't know how Gwenny is around kids."

Marc nodded. "Will do."

Back in his apartment, Marc said to the dog, "Gwenny, want to go meet a five-year-old boy named Charlie? He probably makes a lot of noise, but he won't hurt you. So just stay calm." Gwenny blinked.

Down the stairs they went again. Marc put the slip leash on Gwenny's neck again, they walked to Logan's apartment in the front of the building and knocked on the door.

Charlie threw the door open, saw Gwenny, and squealed. "A dog! Can I pet it?" Charlie was grinning from ear to ear and bouncing up and down on his toes.

Marc knelt down. "Charlie, this dog is scared of everything. So you have to be very quiet and very gentle so she won't get scared."

"I can be quiet."

Logan appeared from the kitchen, and put his hand on Charlie's shoulder. "Hey, Marc. Let's find out if the dog is safe around kids."

"I've never seen any sign of aggression. She just tries to hide if she's scared. And she's scared most of the time." He looked down at Gwenny. She had moved closer to him and was standing half-way behind him now. He could feel her against his legs. She was trembling.

Logan turned to Charlie. "Let's go slowly, son. She's very afraid of everything so let's approach her together." And they did just that. They knelt down, and Logan reached out his hand to begin stroking Gwenny on her head. She accepted his pets. No growling. Charlie was next. "Don't be scared of me, doggy. I won't hurt you," he said in a low, soft voice, almost a whisper. Gwenny accepted his pets, too. Marc felt her stop trembling.

"This is going really well," Marc said. "But I'm keeping her near me until we all get to know each other better. Can we sit on the sofa?"

"Sure. Want anything to drink?" Logan asked.

"I could use another coffee. I'm just here to catch up with you."

Marc sat on the sofa, still holding Gwenny's leash. After a minute, she lowered herself to the carpet next to him, her head up and eyes watching everything.

A large cat came around from behind the sofa. He stopped short when he saw Gwenny. When Gwenny lifted her head, the cat arched his back and hissed. Gwenny blinked.

Marc chuckled. "I think your cat isn't too happy about having a dog in his house. Gwenny doesn't seem interested."

"That's Shevek," Charlie said.

"Yes, he's named after the protagonist in Ursula Le Guin's sci-fi book, *The Dispossessed*," Logan said. "Shevek sleeps a lot."

Shevek turned and stalked away. The next time Marc saw him, the cat was on Charlie's bed.

"What's her name?" Charlie asked. He was sitting on a nearby chair.

"Gwenny. She came all the way from Morocco."

"Where's Morocco? Is that in Oklahoma? My teacher showed us Oklahoma on the map."

"No. Morocco is much farther away. Get a map, and I'll show you."

Charlie jumped down and ran to his bedroom. He came back with a map just as Logan brought cups of coffee for Marc and himself.

Marc took a sip of coffee, opened the world map, and found North Africa. "Here's Morocco," he said. "And on this map, you can see we had to fly across the Atlantic Ocean, then over this part of America, including Oklahoma, to arrive in Arizona. So you can see, we came from a long way away."

Charlie nodded. He slipped down to the floor and came to sit next to Gwenny's long body. The dog looked at him but didn't move.

"This is going well," Marc said to Logan. "Thanks for the coffee."

"Yes, Charlie, you're doing a good job. I think Gwenny is getting used to you. Just don't make any loud noises or any sudden movements," Logan said.

"Okay," Charlies said. He reached out his hand and began to stroke Gwenny's back and hips. The dog looked at him. "I love you, Gwenny," he whispered. After a few minutes, Gwenny put her head down between her front paws and closed her eyes.

"She likes being petted," Marc said. "Look. She's all relaxed and going to sleep. I'll tell Angela about this." He turned to Logan. "Looks like you've had some changes since I've been gone. So Li and Frida are still here. The new gal Xochi is moving in soon. And the one I haven't met is Zoey."

"Zoey's grocery shopping now. She'll be back soon," Logan said. "You'll like her. Zoey is a biology teacher at the high school."

"Zoey and I go on bug hunts and bird hunts. Zoey taught me how to be quiet. You have to be quiet, especially on a bird hunt," Charlie said. He returned to stroking Gwenny.

Logan chuckled. "Yeah, Zoey's turned Charlie into a scientist. A quiet scientist."

"I emailed Nina before I came home. She told me about the shooter who was after her and her band members. She also told me an FBI agent was staying in her apartment for a while, and he ended up bringing down a money-laundering scheme and a dog-fighting ring as well as rescuing Dylan."

"Yeah, that's Cass. You'll probably meet him. I think he and Dylan will be here tomorrow for the potluck."

"Is there anything else I need to know?"

"No, I don't think so." Logan took a sip of coffee. "But there is something I'd like to discuss."

"What's that?"

"This incident that occurred yesterday with your vet and that dude vandalizing her van," Logan started.

"Yeah, I've been worrying about that. Not just because I really like Angela. Something doesn't seem right."

"Despite all what happened with Dylan and Nina and Cass, this neighborhood is usually pretty quiet. It's rare for vehicles here to be vandalized like that. If there is any kind of damage, it's usually some punk doing it to several cars, not just one. I mean like tearing off windshields one car after another, or punching a hole not in just one tire but in several cars' tires. But to have all four tires slashed like that on only one vehicle seems more like the van was targeted. What do you think?" Logan asked.

"Actually, it's a relief to hear you say this. I was thinking the exact same thing. But I know I can be a little on the paranoid side. When I was working these past months, we were always on the lookout for threats. Always."

"I bet you saw a lot of bad stuff. I never figured you would be a photojournalist covering war zones."

"Me, neither. I think I was lured by the excitement and the money. But it turned out that the money wasn't all that great, and the excitement meant either watching people get killed or dodging bullets myself. I finally just quit, and I'll never do that again. I'm looking for something different now, but I'm not sure what I'll do next."

"What do you know about Angela? Could she have an enemy? Or do you think her veterinary practice might be a target?"

"Angela has only been in Tucson for a couple of months. She came here from the New Orleans area. I don't know anything about her veterinary practice, but I think I'm going to ask her more questions about it, and see if anything weird is going on there. She'll be back tomorrow afternoon because she's interested in something called "behavioral health" for dogs. She wants to help Gwenny get over her terror of everything and everybody. Angela thinks Gwenny has been traumatized somehow. Looks like Charlie might be helpful, too." He looked down at Charlie who was still gently stroking Gwenny.

Logan nodded. "Okay, let's stay in touch about this. Meanwhile, I'm contacting the owner of Casa Pacifica apartments and see if they will approve installation of security cameras. The cop made me realize I should have done this earlier."

"I could probably help you with camera installation and setting up the tech end so you can see what's on the video that the camera records."

"Great! I'll make sure you get paid for your work. And if Dr. Brooks, Angela, is going to be here tomorrow afternoon, ask her to come to the potluck tomorrow evening."

"I'll do that." Marc stood up. Gwenny woke up and looked at him. "Thank you so much, Logan. It's great to see you again and it's great to be home."

"Yes, I'm glad you're home, too."

The two men gave each other a quick hug.

"And thank you, Charlie, for helping Gwenny to relax and not be so afraid."

"Can I do that again sometime? Please. Please." Charlie grinned.

"You bet. Come on, Gwenny." Marc said goodbye and led his dog on her leash out the door and back to his apartment. He had to carry her up the stairs again.

4 SURVEILLANCE

Much to Marc's surprise, Logan showed up at his door early Saturday afternoon. Charlie was with him.

"Hey, come on in. What's that, Charlie?" He pointed to a ball in Charlie's hand.

"I want to see if Gwenny wants to play ball." Charlie peered around Marc to see if he could spot Gwenny.

"Okay. Let me talk to your dad first, and then we'll see if Gwenny will play with you."

Logan nodded. "I called the owners of Casa Pacifica after you left this morning. Or to be specific, I talked to the guy who does what he called 'security.' He was all in on installing surveillance cameras on our property. He said they've been doing that on some of their other properties, and just haven't gotten around to us yet. But when he heard about what happened with Angela and her van, and Xochi, too, he said we need to prioritize this."

"That's great to hear."

"We discussed it and decided to put up cameras in the front, on the side entrance, and at the back door into the fenced area. The front and side entrances get priority because they are easy for anyone to access. He sent me out to a local store, and I bought the equipment."

"Does that include connecting the cameras to your wi-fi so you can see what the camera sees?"

"Yes, I bought the correct cameras. The salesman called them IP cameras, which I learned means internet protocol, and also, I got the connection which is called an NVR system. He said it will send the video to me via wi-fi so I can watch on my computer in my apartment. You said you know how to install this?"

"Yes, I installed a system for that friend of mine the last time I was in Tucson."

"So do you think you'd have time to work on this? The security manager said he'd pay you."

"Yes, time is all I have these days."

"Excellent. Then after Charlie tries out the ball on Gwenny, let's go back to my apartment and I'll turn over this equipment to you. We have a ladder out in the shed in the back yard. Do you have any tools?"

"Yes, I have everything I need. Thanks for giving me this opportunity. I need something to do, something useful."

"Thank *you*, Marc. This surveillance system will make us all safer."

Logan turned to Charlie. "Okay, Charlie, let's try our plan."

Charlie giggled. "Okay!"

"You sit here on the floor, and I'll go over there. Want to play?" Logan asked Marc.

"Sure. What do I do?"

"Sit on the floor kind of close to Gwenny while she's in her crate but not super close. We're going to roll the ball around to each other. We're hoping that when the ball goes past Gwenny, she'll show some interest," Logan explained.

Marc nodded, and all three took their places.

They rolled the ball back and forth among the three of them. Charlie was giggling the whole time. "Look,

Gwenny," he said, "you can play, too." Gwenny looked at Charlie when he said her name.

Finally, after several rolls across the floor, Logan aimed the ball to go right past the entrance of Gwenny's crate. When she saw it coming toward her, she lunged forward out of her crate, and she grabbed the ball in her mouth. Charlie clapped and giggled. Then Gwenny just stood there. She didn't know what to do.

Marc took the ball from Gwenny's mouth and rolled it back to Charlie. "Try rolling it to her, and let's see what she does." Charlie complied. Gwenny was still standing outside the crate. She grabbed the ball in her mouth again. They tried this several times, and every time, Gwenny grabbed the ball.

"Try calling her," Marc said.

Charlie called her name several times. Gwenny stared at Charlie, but she didn't move.

"I guess the next step is to get her to bring the ball to you, Charlie," Marc said. "We can work on that."

Logan stood up. "We have to go, but I think we can say that Gwenny knows how to play ball now. Sort of."

Marc turned to Charlie. "Thanks, Charlie! When Angela gets here, we'll play ball again."

"Can I pet Gwenny?" Charlie asked.

"Slowly, quietly," Logan said.

Charlie approached the big dog one step at a time, saying in a quiet voice, "I love you, Gwenny." When he arrived at the dog's side, he stroked Gwenny's head.

"Well done, son. Time to go," Logan said.

As they were leaving the apartment, Marc heard Charlie say, "Daddy, can we get a dog?"

Logan turned back to Marc, rolled his eyes, and said, "Thanks a lot, Marc."

Marc laughed.

* * *

Logan sat in his apartment waiting for Zoey. Charlie was taking a nap. The three of them were going to a baseball game in the evening to see the Arizona Wildcats team play some other team. Logan couldn't remember which team. He liked going to the games even though baseball wasn't his favorite sport. Basketball would always be his first choice, but he enjoyed going with Charlie and Zoey to any athletic event because they both were enthusiastic fans. Going with them was almost like a family outing. Even so, the idea of "family" was scary to Logan. After his wife died, he didn't know if he'd ever have a family again. Then Zoey appeared in their lives, and everything changed.

He heard an odd sort of noise at his door, as if something were being pushed against the door. He went to look. When he opened the door, Zoey was standing there holding several bags of groceries in her arms. She couldn't even reach the door knob, despite having dropped at least one bag. He picked up the bag.

"Oh, great! You're here. Thanks, Logan." She came in, went to the kitchen and unloaded her bags onto the floor.

"What's all this?"

She turned and grinned at him. "I'm going to cook!"

Logan laughed. "Fine by me." He helped her put everything away.

"Go sit on the sofa, Logan Reid. I have a surprise for you."

He did as instructed. When she came to sit with him, she held something in her hand and her hand was pressed against her chest.

"You have to guess what I have."

"I don't have to guess. I know. You have the most beautiful breasts in the world."

Zoey laughed. "No, silly. Try again. What do I have in my hand?"

"A philosophy book?"

"No. Try again."

"A burrito."

"You're hopeless." She stretched out one hand and gave him a bar of Ghirardelli chocolate.

"Oh, wow." Logan turned and looked at Charlie's bedroom door. "Charlie's asleep. I don't have to share." He grinned. "Thank you!" He tore open the paper cover and took a bite. "Yum."

"What have you been doing?" Zoey asked.

"Nothing. Just sitting here thinking."

"You think too much." She chuckled.

Logan took another bite and grinned. He immediately remembered the first time she'd said that to him, only a couple of weeks or so earlier. "You think too much," she'd said. Charlie was spending the night at his friend Javie's home. Logan had asked Zoey out on a date that evening. He dressed in a suit and tie, and she wore a lovely evening gown. They went to a ball, a fundraiser for the Tucson Museum of Art. The head of the Philosophy Department at the University of Arizona where Logan was earning his PhD had invited him, and Logan invited Zoey. Logan felt rather uncomfortable being around all those obviously wealthy people. He had little in common with them. But Zoey looked so good that he stopped thinking about anyone else at the ball. He could only think about her and how beautiful she was.

When they returned home, Logan took Zoey to her apartment door and kissed her goodnight. He went back to his apartment, took off his suit jacket and loosened his tie. He started pacing around his living room, thinking. He wanted Zoey. That's all he could think about. He wanted her. He walked around in a circle thinking about the pull between fear of involvement with her versus the desire he felt for her. If he made love to her, would she die like his first wife, Caroline, had died? But if he didn't make love to her, would he be the one who died from unrequited desire? He decided to go talk to Zoey. Yeah. Tell her what he was thinking.

Logan returned to her apartment door and knocked softly. "Zoey, it's me." She opened the door, took his hand and pulled him inside. She closed and locked the door behind him.

"Zoey, I've been thinking…" He didn't know what to say. She was standing there dressed in pajama shorts and a t-shirt. It was obvious to Logan that she had nothing on under the t-shirt. He felt hot all over.

"Yeah, I've been thinking…" he started.

"Yes?"

"Uh…well…hmmm…uh…yeah…so…I've been thinking…"

Zoey laughed. "Logan, you know what your problem is?"

"What?"

"You think too much." She quickly stripped off her t-shirt and ran to him. Suddenly Logan couldn't breathe. She was kissing him and unbuttoning his shirt and pulling him toward her bedroom. That's when Logan Reid stopped thinking.

Logan laughed and took another bite of chocolate.

"What's funny?"

"I was remembering the first time you told me that I think too much."

Zoey grinned. "That turned out well."

"Yeah, except now we're sneaking around all the time trying to find a few minutes alone so Charlie doesn't catch us doing the deed."

"Doing the deed?" She laughed again.

"Want a bite of chocolate?"

She leaned forward and took a tiny bite.

"Actually, Zoey, I wanted to tell you something important. Marc is going to install a surveillance system so we can see if anyone is lurking around or tries to break in. I want you to learn how to access the information, too."

"That's good. I think it's a good idea, really. You never know who might try to break in. And when Charlie gets older, he's going to want to go outside in the yard by himself. We can keep an eye on him and make sure no one tries to bother him."

They both heard a noise.

"Charlie's awake," Zoey said.

Logan nodded and quickly ate the last bite of chocolate.

* * *

Marc spent the rest of Saturday afternoon installing the cameras and showing Logan how to access the videos and live feed via his wi-fi. Zoey and Charlie were out bird watching. Marc and Logan sat together at Logan's desk, situated at the far end of his living room. Marc switched the view back and forth between the three cameras he had installed.

Logan nodded. "This is good. I should have asked for this a long time ago."

Unexpectedly, they could see a woman with a blonde pony tail approaching the front door. Charlie was right behind her.

"Hey, who's that good looking gal? She's hot. And is that your boy Charlie?"

"That's Zoey. Don't get any ideas about Zoey, Marc. She's *my* good looking gal. And yes, that's Charlie. They've been bird watching this afternoon."

"Don't worry. I won't move in on your territory. Anyway, my territory these days is Dr. Angela Brooks. I'm totally enamored with her."

"Yes, she's very beautiful and seems to be a really good person, too."

Marc nodded just as Zoey and Charlie came in.

Charlie ran up to Marc and said, "Where's Gwenny?"

"She's upstairs taking taking a nap."

"I hope she wakes up."

Marc chuckled. "Don't worry. She'll wake up. You'll see her again."

Logan gestured to Marc. "Zoey, this is Marc Tomassone. I told you about him already. Marc is a long-term resident of Casa Pacifica, but he's been gone the past several months. He's the one with the dog."

Zoey stuck out her hand and smiled. "I'm Zoey Corban. Charlie talked to me a lot about your dog."

"Gwenny!" Charlie said. He wandered off to his bedroom saying, "Gwenny, Gwenny," in a sing-song voice.

"Yes, he was very good with Gwenny. She's afraid of everyone and everything, but Charlie managed to convince her that he's safe because he was so quiet and gentle with her. Logan tells me you're taking Charlie on outings and teaching him how to be quiet."

"Yes, I'm a biology teacher. Charlie is getting better and better at bird identification, and he has learned to be quiet so as to not scare the birds. That's good to hear that he was quiet with your dog, too."

"Zoey, come and take a look," Logan said. He stood up, and Zoey took his place in the chair at the desk. Logan showed her how to access the surveillance cameras. "We can also look at a video of what happened when we haven't been watching."

"Oh, look!" Zoey said. "There are two guys. What are they doing?"

Marc came closer and looked, too.

"Hey, isn't that the guy that came with the tow truck to get Angela's van?" Marc said.

"Yeah," Logan answered. "What's he doing here? And who is that other man?"

"I have no idea," Marc answered.

Both men were dressed in jeans and dark hoodies, both hoodies pulled up over their heads.

"They look like they're sneaking around," Zoey said. "This one…"

"He told us his name is Eric," Logan said.

"He jiggled the front door to see if he could get in," she continued. "He didn't bother knocking or ringing the door bell."

"Yeah, I've been locking it early every evening. I started doing that when we had all that trouble with Nina being stalked." Logan was frowning now. "Look! Now they are going around to the side of the house to see if they can get in through the kitchen door. What the hell?"

"And the other guy is looking over the back fence to see if there's an entrance there," Marc said. "I think they are trying to see if they can get in the apartment building without alerting anyone. This is not good."

"No. Not good." Logan was becoming increasingly alarmed. "Come on, Marc. Let's go have a little chat with these dudes. Zoey, please stay here, and don't let Charlie follow me out."

Zoey nodded. "Be careful."

Logan and Marc headed down the hall to the side entrance of the building. They entered the small kitchenette and laundry room, and Logan quickly unlocked the door and thrust it open.

The man who called himself Eric jumped back down the stairs to the ground. The other man stood there watching.

Logan stepped out with Marc right behind him.

"What are you doing here?" Logan said in a harsh tone.

"Uh. Well." Eric seemed to be at a loss for words. The other man stepped forward and said, "We wanted to know if there's an apartment for rent here."

Bullshit, Marc said silently to himself.

"I find that hard to believe," Logan said. "I'm the apartment manager. If you want to rent, you should contact me directly through the realtor's website. Or you could try knocking on the front door," he added sarcastically.

Marc looked at the other man. He bore a striking resemblance to Eric Carlson. Marc wondered if they were brothers or maybe cousins.

"So you don't have any apartments for rent?" Eric's companion asked.

"What's your name?" Logan demanded.

"I'm Braden."

Logan nodded. "And you're Eric," he said, looking at Eric. "I remember you when you came to get the van. Looks to me like you two boys were trying to break in here."

"No, no," Eric said hurriedly. "My brother and I are just looking around."

Yeah, Marc thought. Brothers.

"We don't have any apartments for rent now. So you two can just get lost," Logan said. He gestured toward the street.

The two men headed toward the street. Braden turned back and scowled at Logan.

Logan and Marc headed back to Logan's apartment.

Marc spoke first. "Logan, there's something weird about this. We know that Eric works for Angela's veterinary clinic. He's the one who came to get her van to be towed. It seems strange that he, and his brother, too, were trying to break into the apartment building. Why would he want to do that?"

"I won't argue with you about that. It is definitely strange. I have no idea what they were up to. I suggest you have a conversation with Angela about this. Ask her about her veterinary firm, who works there and what each person does, and especially, has anything unusual happened recently at her firm. Have they had any threats, for example? And what does she know about Eric? And his brother."

Marc nodded. "Yes, I'll do that. She's coming over tomorrow afternoon to do a little behavior therapy with Gwenny. One of our goals is to get the dog to go up and down the stairs to my apartment. I'll talk to her then."

"Keep me informed," Logan said.

"I will. I'm going back to my place now."

"Thank you for installing the surveillance cameras," Zoey said. "I already feel safer."

Marc nodded and said goodnight.

5 Sunday Morning

On Sunday morning, Marc woke up feeling much better than when he'd arrived home. The jet lag was wearing off, he had more energy, and his outlook on life had improved somewhat. He went to his kitchen and started making coffee. Gwenny was curled up in her crate, staring at him.

"Come on, Gwenny girl, let's go outside."

Same routine, down the stairs, outside, doggy pee and poop, back up the stairs. Carrying her down was the hard part. Marc hoped he wouldn't slip and fall.

Marc talked to Gwenny as he drank his coffee and made breakfast. Then he put kibble in her food bowl and refilled her water bowl. A shower came next. He shaved the stubble off his face and brushed his hair. Later he'd visit a barber and do something about getting a haircut. When he came out of the bathroom with nothing on but a towel wrapped around his middle, he chuckled when he saw that all the kibble was gone. Gwenny was back in her crate again.

He poured another cup of coffee, and he looked at the clock. Nearly ten. Suddenly, there was a soft knock on his door. He opened the door, and much to his surprise, Angela was standing there. Her bicycle was downstairs pushed up again the stair railing, and her helmet was strapped to the bike. Angela had a worried look on her face, for a moment anyway. Her eyebrows went up as her eyes roamed over his bare chest.

"Oh, I'm sorry," she said in a low voice. "Did I interrupt your shower?"

"No, no problem. I just hadn't bothered to put on my clothes yet. I'm surprised to see you. Come on in."

Angela entered Marc's apartment, and she went directly to Gwenny.

"I'll be back in a minute." Marc reappeared five minutes later in dressed jeans and a blue t-shirt.

Gwenny had come out of the crate and was standing still, allowing Angela to stroke her.

"Marc," she looked up at him, "something really wonderful happened. Gwenny wagged her tail when she saw me."

Marc grinned. "That's very good. I have a story to tell you. Gwenny and Charlie and Logan and I played ball yesterday." He filled her in on the details.

"So she went to get the ball, but then she just got stuck? No attempt to return it to Charlie?"

"That's right. She didn't know what to do next."

Angela smiled. "She'll figure it out. It sounds to me like Charlie is quite the dog behavior therapist."

"Only five years old, and he and Gwenny already made a connection." Marc sat down on the sofa. "I thought you weren't coming until this afternoon."

Angela joined him on the sofa. She was frowning now, and she looked very worried. "Something scary happened."

"Tell me."

"Yesterday afternoon, I got off work around noon because my van wasn't ready yet to take out to see clients, and they didn't need me in the clinic. So I went home. But I got a surprise call from a friend who had just arrived in Tucson. Her name is Liz, and she and I worked together for that vet gig on the Native American reservations that I told you about. She was on her way to San Francisco for a wedding, and she had an unexpected layover in Tucson. She called and invited me to go with her to this resort where she stayed last night, La Paloma."

Marc nodded. "I know the place."

"So we spent the afternoon and evening together, I stayed with her last night, we spent most of the time talking, and I saw her off at the airport really early this morning. Then I went home. When the taxi dropped me at my place, I noticed right away that something wasn't right."

"What do you mean?" Marc felt a growing sense of concern.

"Someone had been in my house. Or I should say, my friend's house where I'm house sitting. Somehow the intruder got in the front door. The rug just inside the door was pushed out of the way. Everything in the house was the same except in my bedroom. I could see that drawers had been opened and contents had been disturbed. Not just the chest of drawers. Also things had been moved just a little on several shelves and in the cabinet in the bathroom. Not much had changed. It was very subtle. And even more concerning, there was an impression on my bed and pillow, as if the intruder had been lying down on my bed."

Marc took her hand. "You're very observant."

"One more thing. I left a jar of orange juice in the refrigerator yesterday morning. It was three-quarters full when I left it there. But this morning it was only about one-third full. Someone drank from the jar." She looked at him. "Marc, I'm scared. I don't know anyone here except the people I work with. And you. I don't know the people at the vet clinic very well because we've been too busy to spend any time together. You're the only one I know even a little bit. I hope I'm not bothering you."

"No. Of course not. I'm glad you came to me. I want to help you."

"You do?" She frowned. "Despite the fact that my behavior yesterday was so inappropriate, so unprofessional?"

"What do you mean?"

"I kissed you on your cheek. I'm not supposed to kiss my clients." She paused. "But I like you." She looked close to tears.

Marc smiled. "No problem. Of course, I can always take back that kiss."

Angela looked at him. "Take it back? I don't understand."

Marc leaned toward her and kissed her on her lips. "There. I just took back your kiss. And I'm not your client. Well, yeah, sort of. I'll make sure you get paid. But I'm more than a client. Remember you said I'm a kindred spirit? We're friends now, and I'm going to do my best to keep you safe."

A smile appeared on Angela's face.

"What's with the bicycle? Did you come here from your house on your bike?" Marc asked.

"Yes. I go everywhere on a bicycle. Or the city bus. I don't have a car."

"Oh. Okay. Then we'll use my car." He leaned back against the sofa. "Let me think a minute." Angela was sitting forward, her elbows on her knees. Marc pulled her back to sit close to him.

"Yesterday, I installed surveillance cameras at three locations on our apartment building. Logan arranged for that. We were showing his girlfriend how the cameras work when these two dudes showed up. We watched them on the cameras. They were poking around, and it looked like they were trying to break in. One of the dudes was Eric, that man who works at your vet's office."

"What? I don't understand."

"I don't understand either. I suggest we go talk to Logan because he has a history of figuring out weird things."

"Let's take Gwenny. I want to watch her interact with Charlie."

"Sure. Charlie will love that."

Angela leaned toward Marc and kissed him, this time on his lips. "Thank you, friend."

Marc grinned. "Oh, I'm going to be forced to take back that kiss."

This time his kiss was on her lips again, but the kiss lasted longer. Then there was a second kiss.

Angela was smiling when Marc pulled back.

"Okay," he said. "Let's go downstairs and see Logan."

* * *

After Logan welcomed them into his apartment, Zoey jumped up from the sofa where she was sitting with Charlie reading a book. She cried out, "Angela!" She had a huge grin on her face.

"Zoey!" Angela returned the big smile. The two women came together and hugged each other.

"You two know each other?" Logan asked.

"Yes," Zoey said. "Angela came and talked to the Girls in STEM Club. I'm their faculty sponsor."

"STEM?" Marc asked. "Doesn't that have something to do with science or something."

"Yes, science, technology, engineering and mathematics," Zoey explained. "It's a club for girls who think they'd like to go into a STEM field. Angela told us all about what's it's like to be a veterinarian."

"Meeting with those girls was one of the most fun things I've done since I've been in Tucson."

"Your presentation was great. The girls loved it. They want to invite you back," said Zoey.

"My pleasure," Angela answered with a grin.

Meanwhile, Charlie was slowly and quietly approaching Gwenny. When the dog saw him, Gwenny wagged her tail.

"Daddy, did you see that? Gwenny wagged her tail," Charlie said.

"Yes. You're doing all the right things, son. Looks like Gwenny isn't afraid of you anymore," Logan answered.

"Sorry to interrupt, but Angela and I are hoping you can help us, Logan. Some weird things are happening, and we thought maybe you could help us figure out what to do," Marc said. "Are you busy now?"

"No. You've made me curious."

"Let's get Charlie and Gwenny distracted," Angela said. "Then we can talk." She turned to Charlie. "Do you know what a play bow is?"

"I'm not sure."

"I'll show you." Angela found a photo of a big dog on her cell phone, a Great Dane, in the play bow position. "This is a signal to other dogs that this dog wants to play. You have a ball, right?"

"Yes, I'll go get it." Charlie left and returned about a minute later.

"Marc, take Gwenny over there across the room and take her leash off," Angela said. Marc did as instructed.

"Charlie, now you do a play bow. Make sure Gwenny is looking at you."

Charlie giggled and then did his best to look like a big dog in a play bow.

"Look," Angela pointed to Gwenny. "She wagged her tail. Now roll the ball to her. Slowly."

Charlie did a play bow again, giggling the entire time. Then he rolled the ball toward Gwenny. The dog took one step forward and picked the ball up with her mouth.

"Okay, Charlie. Now you're going to teach her to fetch. She has the ball in her mouth. So you call out 'Fetch, Gwenny. Fetch.'"

Charlie did exactly that. He called out to Gwenny, giggled some more, did another play bow, then called out to her to fetch. After a moment, Gwenny came directly to Charlie and dropped the ball at his feet.

"Oh! Look!" everyone said at the same time.

"Now, Charlie, you and Gwenny are standing together. Roll the ball out a little ways, look at Gwenny, point to the ball, and say, 'fetch' until she goes and picks up the ball and brings it back to you."

Marc noticed immediately that the dog's eyes went to where Charlie was pointing. "I didn't realize that a dog would look at something when we point to it."

"Yes, that ability is called 'point comprehension' or 'point following.' Not many animals can do that, but dogs are good at it."

Gwenny went to the ball and picked it up. Charlie called her back to him, and she came immediately.

"Well done, Charlie," Angela said. "Keep going until you both get tired. Then you two can sit together, and you can pet her."

Charlie grinned. "I like playing fetch, and I like petting Gwenny."

"Logan, your boy is a natural," Angela said. "He could easily learn to train dogs."

Logan nodded and smiled. "Yeah, Charlie's a pretty smart kid." He gestured to his sofa. "So now this looks like a good time for us all to have a chat about what's going on. Let's sit over here." Angela and Marc sat on the sofa facing the big window that looked out on their street, and Zoey and Logan sat in two stuffed chairs facing them.

"I'll start," Marc said. "I told Angela about the new surveillance system here, and how it caught those two guys lurking around yesterday evening. Then Angela came earlier than expected today because of her concern about an intrusion into the house where's she staying."

"Yes, I'm house sitting for a friend. She'll be back soon." Angela described what she'd observed when she arrived home early that morning. "I'm convinced that someone got into the house and was in my bedroom. And also he drank some orange juice from a container in the refrigerator."

"Do you have any idea about what time the intruder got into your house?" Logan asked.

Angela shook her head. "No, not really. I worked at the clinic in the morning, and I returned home about noon. I was with my friend at La Paloma from about two in the afternoon yesterday until early this morning."

"And you feel like you were the target? Not your friend?"

"There were no signs of the intruder being in my friend's bedroom. He was in my bedroom only."

"Nothing was stolen?" Logan asked.

"No. The signs of intrusion were subtle but unmistakable for anyone paying attention. I have the distinct idea that the person wanted me to know someone had been there. Like drinking part of the orange juice. That's hard to miss," she said.

"Do you think someone is trying to intimidate you or scare you by sneaking into your place when you're not there? And if so, why?"

Angela was becoming visibly concerned. "Logan, I just don't know. I haven't lived here very long. I don't have a conflict with anyone. Why would someone want to scare me?"

"Also there's the matter of Eric and his brother showing up here," Marc said. "Do you think that has anything to do with this?"

"Eric and his brother could have simply been hoping to break into one of the apartments so they could steal stuff. But it could be more complicated than that." Logan paused for a moment. "So, Angela, everyone at your vet clinic knew you had yesterday afternoon off because of the van being disabled."

She nodded. "Some of them knew. I don't know if everyone knew."

"Perhaps the intruder thought you would be there at home when he, or she, showed up. But you weren't there. And you didn't come back in the evening. If it was Eric looking for you, he and his brother may have come here to the apartments to see if they could find you."

"I don't know why he would want to visit me at home. He and I rarely even talk to each other. And why he thought I'd be here at Marc's place isn't clear. Also I don't know Eric's brother."

Logan shrugged his shoulders. "It's possible that Eric thought there was a connection between you and Marc. He may have been watching you. Did you tell anyone at work that you were coming here today to see Marc and Gwenny?"

Angela frowned. "As a matter of fact, I did tell one of the other vets that I would be visiting Marc and Gwenny. I told her about my interest in behavioral veterinary work. Her name is Jessica McKinnah."

"Eric may have overheard this conversation. Can you think of anyone else who might have wanted to see you while you're at home?"

"No. I hardly know anyone here in Tucson. I haven't been here that long." Angela paused. "There was one male client who was a little too familiar with me, if you know what I mean."

"Tell me what you mean," Logan asked.

"I mean asking me out and getting a little aggressive when I said no. He tried to kiss me. But I wasn't interested, and I made that clear. Anyway that all happened last month."

Marc was frowning now. "So what about Eric? Has he made any moves on you?"

"No. Not really. Like I said, we don't interact much. He's really rather unfriendly."

Logan nodded. "Yes, that's how I experienced him when he came with the tow truck to take away the van." He paused again. "I suggest you give us a bigger picture. Tell us about your veterinary clinic. And what do you do when you're not working?"

"That last question is the easiest," she said. "I ride my bike around a lot. And I visit Tucson hot spots."

"Hot spots? Like night clubs or something?" Logan asked. "You don't strike me as a nightclub kind of person."

"Oh, no," Angela wrinkled up her nose at the thought of nightclubs. "My favorite place is the Arizona-Sonora Desert Museum. That was a challenge getting there out there. I had to take a bus to the west side of Tucson, then a taxi to the museum. But it was worth it. What a wonderful place! I stayed there all day. Then I was lucky to catch a ride back to town with a family visiting from Santa Fe."

"Any other hot spots?" Logan smiled.

"I've been to the art museum downtown, and I've visited the University of Arizona campus to see the Arizona

State Museum and the Flandrau Science Center. And I went to the Tucson Botanical Gardens and a Japanese garden not far away. Yume Japanese Garden. That's the name."

"So you are visiting cultural sites."

"That's right. I don't have a car so I go to places I can get to on my bike or on the city bus."

"There are more places that you would really enjoy," Marc said. "I'd like to show you."

Angela looked at him and smiled. "I'll take you up on that. Thank you."

"So tell us about your veterinary clinic and your colleagues," Logan said.

"The head of the clinic is Dr. Ted Wilden. He owns the practice. The other vets are Federico Varo, we call him Freddy, and there's Jessica and me. We have an office manager and receptionist, Carol Wilson, and two veterinary assistants. One is Lexie Garcia. She helps the doctors during exams, cares for animals after surgery or in emergencies, and gives out medications and immunizations. Eric does those same tasks sometimes, but he is usually stuck with the not-so-fun jobs like cleaning cages, running errands, and arranging tow trucks for damaged mobile vet vans."

"And you haven't had any conflicts with any of these people?" Logan asked.

"No. We don't see each other all that much because we're so busy. And I'm gone a lot in the mobile vet van. But everyone is friendly. Well, except Eric. He's not especially friendly with anyone."

Logan was quiet for a few minutes. "I'd like to think about this a little bit."

"Sure. Anyway you can help would be great," Angela said.

"Meanwhile, we're having the potluck this evening."

"Oh, gosh," Marc said. "Angela, let's see if we can come up with something to bring to the potluck."

Angela grinned. "Sure!"

"I should mention, too," Logan said. "one of the people who'll be here at the potluck is Cass Cosay. He used to be an FBI Special Agent, and he might have some insight. Meanwhile, try to remember if anything else has happened, Angela. I mean at your clinic, or with visits to clients in your mobile van, or while you're alone. There may be something else going on that will give us a clue."

Angela nodded. "Thank you, Logan."

Marc stood, found the slip leash, and called Gwenny. She and Charlie were curled up against each other on the rug, and Charlie was stroking Gwenny. The dog looked like she was in heaven. He went to them, slipped the leash over Gwenny's head, and said, "Come on, Dr. Brooks. Let's go back to my place and see what we can come up with for the potluck."

They said their goodbyes.

Charlie came to sit with Logan and Zoey.

"Daddy, can we get a dog?"

"I have an idea," Zoey said. "I bet Marc would like a break every now and then. How about we ask him if he'd like to share Gwenny with us? Kind of what the courts call 'joint custody.' We'll have her sometime, and Marc will have her sometime. What do you think?"

"I think that's a great idea, Zoey. What do you think, Charlie?" Logan smiled and nodded. The idea of taking on a dog full-time seemed like a lot of extra work right now. Part-time was better.

"I like it. Gwenny could stay here with me a lot, and we could play together."

"Okay," Logan said. "I'll talk to Marc about this."

Charlie went off to his room.

Logan turned to Zoey. "I think Marc and Angela really like each other." He grinned.

"That's obvious," Zoey chuckled.

"Not as much as I like you," Logan said.

"Oh, yeah?"

He leaned over and kissed her. "Want to do the deed?"

Zoey laughed. "Not now! Later."

"I'll hold you to that, Zoey Corban."

6 Sunday Potluck

"Let's try the stairs again," Angela said.

"You'll need a whole roasted chicken to get Gwenny to go up the stairs," Marc said. "This staircase is much bigger than the one leading to your porch."

"Then let's get Charlie to help us."

They knocked on Logan's door again and asked for Charlie. He was enthusiastic about helping. He went to find his ball, then joined them. Logan and Zoey joined them, too. Charlie ran up the stairs to the landing, turned, and called for Gwenny. She was alert now. Charlie pulled the ball out and called to her, "Gwenny, come and get the ball. Come on, Gwenny."

Marc removed the slip leash from her neck. The dog was staring intently at Charlie and twitching. Marc laughed. "She wants to do it. She wants to get that ball."

Suddenly, Gwenny took off. Up the stairs she went in a flash. She pushed up against Charlie and licked his face. Then she grabbed the ball from his hands. Charlie was laughing uncontrollably. He rolled over onto his back, giggling the entire time. He grabbed the ball back from Gwenny and threw it down the stairs.

"Go get it, Gwenny. Go get the ball!" Charlie giggled.

Down the stairs the greyhound went, super fast, skipping steps as she made it to the first floor. She grabbed the ball and stood there staring at Charlie, her tail wagging.

"Fetch," Charlie called out. "Fetch the ball, Gwenny."

Up the stairs the dog went again, and she nudged Charlie. He took the ball from her mouth and hugged her. "You're so smart, Gwenny. I love you, Gwenny."

"Do you still have that dog biscuit I gave you?" Angela asked. Charlie nodded yes. "Give it to her for fetching."

Charlie gave Gwenny the dog biscuit. Crunch. Crunch. Tail wagging.

"You'd make a very good behavioral therapy veterinarian," Angela said to Charlie.

Charlie nodded. "When I grow up, I'm going to be an ornithologist and study birds, and I'm going to be a veterinarian and take care of dogs, and cats, too. And I'm going to be a philosopher like my daddy."

This surprised Logan, and pleased him greatly, although he wasn't sure Charlie even knew what a philosopher does. Or what philosophy is, for that matter.

"What does a philosopher do, Charlie?" Zoey asked. She was smiling.

"Philosophers think about things," Charlie answered.

Logan looked at Zoey. She was biting her lip, trying to not laugh. He felt his face get hot, and most likely, red. So annoying to blush so easily. He knew that Zoey was thinking about the first time she'd told him that he'd been thinking too much.

"Sorry to disturb," Marc said, "but Angela and I need to come up with something edible for the potluck. See you later." He and Angela went up the stairs, and Marc put the slip leash on Gwenny again.

"See you this evening," Logan called out.

When they arrived at Marc's door, Angela said, "Here's the real test." She slipped a dog biscuit into his hand.

"You go down the stairs and see if you can get her to go down to you. I'll follow."

Marc descended the stairs, held up the dog biscuit, and said, "Come, Gwenny. Come." The dog went down the stairs in a flash, Angela was right behind her.

"Let's go outside and see if she needs to pee," Angela said. They went out, Gwenny did her business, then they were back at the foot of the stairs again.

"I'll go up first," Marc said.

"No dog biscuit this time," Angela said.

Much to their great satisfaction, Gwenny went right up the stairs. She was rewarded with gentle strokes and words of praise.

"I'm very pleased about this," Marc said.

"Problem solved!" Angela said. She threw her arms around Marc and kissed him.

Marc stepped back in mock horror. "Take it back! Take it back!"

Angela laughed. She pulled him to her and kissed him ardently. She let him go and grinned. "Now stop messing with me. Let's come up with something to take to the potluck."

Marc laughed. "I think you are the one who is messing with me, Dr. Brooks."

After surveying Marc's empty cabinets and refrigerator, they decided to take a walk down to the closest grocery store. They bought bananas, apples, kiwi, blueberries, and strawberries. Back in Marc's apartment, they made a fruit salad in a big bowl. As evening neared, they went to Logan's apartment for the traditional Sunday evening potluck. Marc led Gwenny on her leash, and Angela carried the fruit salad.

Logan opened the door wide. "Come on in." He turned to the others in the room and said, "Hey, everybody. Here's Marc Tomassone. Finally, he's home! And his companions are veterinarian Dr. Angela Brooks, and this is Gwenny, Marc's dog."

Charlie came out of his room, dropped to his knees and slid across the hardwood floor toward Gwenny. He threw his arms around the dog who was wagging her tail. "Come on, Gwenny. Come with me, and we'll play." Charlie and Gwenny disappeared into Charlie's room.

Logan continued, "Marc, you know Li and Zoey. Frida is away at a union conference. You've met Xochi. She hasn't actually moved in yet. And this is Dylan Scott and Cass Cosay. They were both living here, but now they live up north near Whiteriver. They're here this weekend to move the rest of their stuff to their new home."

Dylan smiled and waved. Cass stood up and shook Marc's hand. "Good to meet you," Cass said.

"Likewise," Marc responded. "I'm really glad to be home."

Cass shook hands with Angela. "Dr. Brooks," he said.

"Call me Angela, please."

Cass nodded.

"Zoey and I have been roasting two chickens, but they aren't quite ready yet. So feel free to talk your heads off, or play ball with Charlie and Gwenny, or whatever," Logan said.

"Logan said you'd like to talk with me," Cass said.

"Yes, I hope you don't mind. We have sort of a mystery to deal with, and nothing makes much sense."

"Yeah, I was an FBI Special Agent for several years so I have some experience with trying to make sense of things. How about if we go outside where we won't be interrupted?"

* * *

Cass, Angela, and Marc went out into the side yard and sat in lawn chairs under a big mesquite tree.

"Logan just gave me a general idea about your problem, but I'd rather hear everything from you in as much detail as possible," Cass said.

"I just got back to Tucson," Marc said. "I brought the dog with me. It's kind of hard to believe now, but the dog was scared to death of everything and trembling constantly. Now Charlie's her best friend, and they like to play together. Anyway, so I called a vet who would come over and check out Gwenny so I wouldn't have to to take her to a vet's office where she would be terrified. Angela showed up."

"I am with a veterinary clinic that has a mobile unit. I spend most of the week visiting people's homes to care for their animals," Angela added.

Marc went on to tell Cass about the mysterious man who had vandalized Angela's van, and punched both Angela and Xochi in their faces when the two women confronted him before he ran off. "Eric, who works at Angela's vet clinic, came the next day and arranged for the van to be towed away. Meanwhile, Logan decided to have surveillance cameras installed here at Casa Pacifica, and I did the installation. That's when we saw Eric with his brother on the surveillance camera. This was Saturday evening. We think those two were trying to break in to our apartment building."

"And you confronted them?"

"Logan confronted them. They claimed to be looking for a place to rent. Logan ended up emphatically telling them to leave the property. So they left."

Cass smiled. "Logan always seems like such a mild-mannered guy, but he won't take any shit off anyone." He was quiet for a moment. "So Logan told me, Angela, that you only worked this past Saturday morning, then you went with a friend to stay overnight at La Paloma. And when you returned, you found that someone had broken into your place."

"Yes. I was supposed to come this afternoon to Marc's place to help with Gwenny, but when I returned home early this morning and found that someone had been there, I came early to see Marc because I was scared."

"Good idea. So now tell me about your veterinary practice."

Angela gave Cass an overview of the four veterinarians who worked at the clinic, as well as the office manager and the two veterinary assistants.

"So this fellow Eric is a vet assistant, but he does most of the clean up work, labor intensive jobs, and the like?" Cass asked. "Why does Lexie get to do the jobs that are more professional, like helping the doctors in surgeries, doing preliminary exams, and tasks like that?"

"Lexie is just smarter and more capable. And she's better educated. Eric is kind of slow. He just isn't really up to Lexie's level. Also she's friendly to the clients and tries to reassure them. Eric is taciturn and rarely smiles."

"Does anyone at your practice have a police record?"

"Gosh, I don't know," Angela answered. "I haven't been there very long. I don't know very many people here in Tucson, and I don't know the folks at my vet clinic very well."

"Text me the names of everyone, and I'll check with my former colleagues about any police records. Someone came to your place and broke in while you were gone Saturday afternoon. Normally you wouldn't have been there because you would have been working. Instead you were with a friend. So it could have been anyone. Any thief off the street."

"Yes, but nothing was stolen. And I have the distinct feeling that the intruder wanted me to know that they had been there. Drinking my orange juice made it all a bit obvious."

Cass frowned. "This all suggests that intimidation is the goal, not theft. Logan thinks maybe that the intruder might have been Eric. He knew you weren't working Saturday afternoon, he didn't know about your friend visiting, and when he didn't find you at home, he came looking for you here at Casa Pacifica. That's when he and his brother were caught on surveillance."

"If Eric was trying to find me when I was away from the vet clinic, I don't know why. He and I have barely spoken to each other."

"Do you think he wants something from you? Or maybe he wants to confront you about something? Or, as I said, does he want to intimidate you for some reason?"

"I don't know. I just don't know."

"Okay. Let's go back to your vet practice. Have you had any contentious interactions with clients lately?"

"No. Not at all. My clients are happy with my work."

"Wait," Marc interrupted. "What about that guy you said was hassling you?"

"Oh, yeah. His name is Derek. He has nine dogs. I checked them all out and gave them up-to-date vaccinations. As I was leaving, he said he wanted to see me again, and he grabbed me and tried to kiss me. I pushed him away, and I could tell it pissed him off. I guess he was accustomed to getting his way with women, but that manhandling stuff doesn't work with me."

"Have you heard from him again?"

"He called our office and asked for another visit, but this time, Freddy, the other male vet, went out to Derek's place. Freddy said his visit was brief. He found it amusing that Derek seemed disappointed that Freddy showed up, not me. Since then, I haven't heard from Derek."

"What about anything happening at the vet's office? Any confrontations with clients or among the workers or anything?"

Angela paused. "Not really. The only thing I can think of is this. One afternoon about a week ago, I came back to the office a little early. I was in the room next to Ted's office. That's Ted Wilden. He's the director of our clinic, and the owner, too. His wife had come in, and they were having a big argument. Her name is Phoebe. They were yelling at each other, but the door was closed so I couldn't make out most of what they were saying. Then she opened the door and yelled at him. "You better tell me who she is or there will be hell to pay." She stomped out, slamming the door behind her."

"Well, that sounds like a jealous wife," Cass said. "Do you know anything about Dr. Ted's extracurricular love life?"

"No, I haven't heard anything about that. I don't know how he could be seeing someone. He's really busy at our clinic." Angela turned to Marc. "I'm sorry, Marc. I didn't tell you about this. I guess I was just thinking about myself."

"That's totally understandable," Marc said. "You were scared."

"Anything else?" Cass asked.

"I'm not there at the office very much so if there have been problems with any of the clients or among my coworkers, I don't know about it." Angela paused. "There is one other thing that has happened recently, but I doubt it's relevant."

Cass smiled. "You'd be surprised. Tell me more."

"We often have to give our patients an injection of one of the drugs used as a painkiller or sedative. Recently, Lexie and all the vets, that includes me, have been complaining about one of the painkillers not being as strong as in the past. Dr. Ted even contacted the manufacturer to complain, but the manufacturer says they haven't changed the composition of the drug at all."

"Give me a general overview about the drugs you use in your practice, and in particular, any opioid-related drugs," Cass said.

"Mostly we use NSAIDS which is short for 'nonsteroidal anti-inflammatory drugs.' We use them for some simple surgeries and for treatment of arthritis and complaints like that. As far as opioid-related, we do have a supply of a drug called hydromorphone. It's an opioid which we use to knock out an animal for a more lengthy surgery required to treat severe injuries. And we use it for post-surgical pain. But too much of it can kill our animal patients."

"And can kill humans, too, I bet," Marc said.

Cass nodded.

"We also have to avoid interactions with other drugs that a dog is taking, and some dogs have other preexisting medical issues that dictate not using this drug. Oh, yeah. I should have mentioned that only dogs get this drug. It's contraindicated for cats. Hydromorphone is bad for the cat's central nervous system."

"How about human animals?" Marc asked.

"Bad idea," Angela frowned. "It's two to eight times stronger than morphine. And there's a real risk for addiction or even death if doses are too high. Hydromorphone is designated as a controlled substance."

"This is all very good information, Angela," Cass said.

"So my irrelevant comment might have some relevance?"

"Yes, definitely," Cass nodded. "Is the room with the medications kept locked? And who has access to it?"

"Yes, it's always locked. And we all have access to it."

"Back to this guy who was bothering you, Derek? Did he ask for any pain-killer medications for his dogs?"

"No. That didn't come up at all."

"Okay. And who is responsible for the medications at your vet's office? I mean who keeps track of the supply and who restocks."

"Lexie keeps a record of the supply, and she reorders when we're low on a particular medication. Eric restocks them when new meds come in. By that I mean, he puts the new vials on the shelves in the correct place."

"Do you have surveillance cameras in your veterinary office?" Cass asked.

"No, not that I know of. If any cameras are there, I haven't noticed them," Angela said.

Marc spoke up. "I think I know where you're going with this, Cass. I can install surveillance cameras."

Cass nodded. "There's a possibility that someone is taking some of that opioid drug and using it or selling it. But if the person who keeps track of inventory hasn't mentioned any missing vials of the drug, then it's possible that someone is siphoning it off."

"What do you mean?" Angela asked.

"There have been cases where someone inserts a hypodermic needle into a vial of the drug, removes the contents using a syringe, and moves the contents to an empty vial. Then he reinserts the needle into the original vial and fills it to the top with saline solution. But in this case, your vets have found that the drug still works, but it's weak and not as effective. So perhaps just a portion is being removed. If that is done with several vials, the drug thief could end up with a substantial amount of stolen drug, in this case hydromorphone. He goes home with vials filled with the opioid drug."

"And surveillance cameras would be the way to catch them?" Angela asked.

Cass nodded. "Technically speaking, you really should get permission from the owner of the veterinary practice to install surveillance cameras. But you don't know who might be stealing the drug. The most likely ones are either Lexie or Eric, but there's an outside possibility that it's one of the vets. One of them might be an addict. So if you asked for permission to install the cameras, you could be tipping off the perpetrator. You'll have to decide if you want to do this, and take the heat if you get caught. Or you could turn all this over to law enforcement. I don't know if they'd be willing to act because there's not much to go on at this point. You have no proof that the drug has been altered. It would be better to catch the thief in the act of siphoning off the opioid drug. And get some of the altered vials tested. That's harder to do because you can't tell by looking which ones have been altered."

"We can do this," Marc said. "I'm very concerned about Angela's welfare. We need to figure out what's going on so she'll be safe."

Cass turned to Marc. "Do you think you can install the cameras secretly? That probably means Angela letting you into the office first, and then into the room with the meds. This would best be done sometime late at night or better yet, really early morning when you would not be observed or worse, encounter the perpetrator. If there's an alarm system, Angela, you may have to disable it and then re-enable it when Marc is done installing the cameras."

"Yes, we can do this," Marc said firmly. "Thank you so much, Cass. You've given us a lot to work with."

"You thought of several approaches and possibilities that I would never have thought of," said Angela.

"Probably that's because you're not a criminal." Cass smiled. "I've known my fair share of criminals during my work at the FBI, and they can get really creative about finding ways to break the law."

Logan came out the side stairs. "The chicken is coming out of the oven now. But before we go in, can you give me a brief summary of what you think, Cass?"

Cass did just that. He concluded with, "You know most crimes are motivated by drugs, sex, or money. Or a combination. In this case, probably it's drugs, and maybe drugs and money together."

Logan nodded. "That all makes sense. Drugs are behind a lot of crime these days. But why is Angela being targeted? Everyone at the clinic can get into the medications room."

"I think I know why," Angela said. "When I'm out late on mobile visits, I don't get back to the clinic until seven or even eight. The clinic has been closed for two or three hours by that time. I've gone into the meds room late a couple of times, and I found Eric there. He always had a broom in hand, and he said he was tidying up."

Cass nodded. "So you are viewed as a potential threat. You could arrive unexpectedly just as he's siphoning the opioid drug off and injecting it into different vials."

"He's trying to intimidate you, Angela. He'd like for you to resign and be gone," Logan said. He stood up. "Time to eat. We'll deal with this later."

Marc took Angela's hand in his and whispered, "I'm with you all the way."

She smiled and squeezed his hand in return.

* * *

They returned to find that dinner was ready. Zoey had just moved the two roasted chickens to the table, and

Logan went to retrieve his carving knife. Li brought a Chinese dish, *jiaozi*, which looked a lot like dumplings. Cass and Dylan contributed a selection of veggies with a hummus dip. And Marc and Angela's fruit salad was added, too.

"Where's the ice cream?" Charlie asked. "Gwenny wants some ice cream."

Zoey chuckled and looked at Logan.

"Not to worry, son. It's in the freezer. Eat your dinner first. And Gwenny can have only one spoonful," Logan answered. He brushed Charlie's tousled blond hair out of his eyes. "We need to get you a haircut," Logan muttered.

After the meal, they all sat in a circle drinking wine and entertaining each other with tales of what they'd been doing. Everyone contributed, even Angela who shared her experiences as a vet in Tucson and also on the Native American reservations. She made a connection with Cass because she'd been to his Fort Apache reservation.

Logan introduced Xochi as their new resident artist, and she gave them a brief introduction to artist's books. Li announced that he got a pay raise at his job, and he'd been approached about doing some cooking videos for Tik Tok and YouTube. "I'm thinking about writing a cookbook, too," Li said.

Cass and Dylan took turns telling them about their project to provide equine therapy. "We'll be working with three different therapists, and sessions will be for military veterans with PTSD, women who have been victims of violent assaults, and for kids on the autism spectrum, too," Cass explained. "We've started building platforms for big tents where they can stay during their week-long sessions," added Dylan.

"We have our horses ready to go, and Tornado and I go for a run every day," Cass grinned. "And best of all, Dylan isn't quite the handful I thought she'd be. She actually listens to me now, and sometimes, she even does what I tell her to do." Dylan giggled. "Cass rewards me for my good behavior." Cass nodded, smiling.

Marc was quiet until someone asked him what he'd been doing. He frowned. "Well, you know I've been working as a freelance photojournalist for some of the big news organizations. Reuters, *The Guardian*, the BBC mostly. And PBS, too. I saw a lot of awful things because I was in several different war zones."

Angela reached out and took his hand. "He's not really ready to talk about that yet."

Marc nodded. "Mostly it was just bombs and blood."

"I was in Afghanistan serving with the U.S. Army. I know what you mean," said Cass.

"I'm going to try to think of some good things that happened, and when I remember those times, I'll share that with you," Marc said.

"Take your time, Marc," Logan said. "Take your time."

Everyone nodded in agreement.

Charlie got his bowl of ice cream, and Gwenny got her spoonful of ice cream. Everyone else finished their wine, and they all said goodnight to each other.

Back in Marc's apartment, Angela said, "Damn, all the men in Casa Pacifica are real hotties."

Marc laughed. "You think so?"

"Yeah, Li and Cass and Logan. All are very good-looking men. And so different. Chinese, Apache Native American, and a white dude with those really cute granny glasses. Two white dudes. You are the hottest one of all."

Marc felt embarrassed and unaccountably pleased. He didn't know what to say.

"Time for me to go home. I have to go to work in the morning."

"I'll take you and your bike home. Gwenny can come with us. And I'm staying at your place tonight, Angela. I can sleep in the other bedroom or on the sofa." His voice was serious now.

"You don't have to do that, Marc."

"No, I don't *have* to do that, but I *want* to do that. So please don't argue with me. I'm staying with you. I want you to be safe."

Angela nodded. "I feel safer just hearing you say this. So I won't argue with you, but I may be forced to take back that kiss. I mean the one you're going to give me before I go to sleep."

Marc laughed. "Okay. I'll go along with that." He turned to Gwenny. "Come on, girl. You can sleep with me tonight. But no kissing."

7 Cameras and Cannoli

Marc loaded Angela's bike onto the bike rack on the roof of his car, and Gwenny went into the back seat. The trip to Angela's house didn't take long. It was well after dark now.

"Give me a minute. I'll turn on the light," Angela said. She found her keys, went up the steps onto the dark porch, unlocked the front door of the house and went inside. A moment later, the porch light came on.

Marc was waiting for Gwenny to pee before they went in the house. As he waited, he noticed something on the outer wall of the house between the door and window. Something sort of dark and blurry, he couldn't tell what. Gwenny finished her business, and she easily mounted the stairs to the front porch.

He quickly realized that what he was seeing was a block of text, handwritten in a dark color that stood out against the adobe-colored wall. The words were too small to see from very far away, but the closer he got, the clearer it became. The letters were messy and sloppy as if they'd been written in a hurry. He drew in a sharp breath when he read the words.

"Get out of town Nigger Bitch."

Angela came out smiling, but when she saw Marc's face, her smile faded. "What's wrong?"

He looked at her. "I'm sorry. I'm so sorry." He redirected his gaze at the racial slur on the wall.

Angela came to his side. Marc heard her gasp. He put his arm around her shoulders.

"Well, how about that?" she said. Marc could hear the fury in her voice.

"Someone wants you out of the way," he said. He felt both anger and a deep concern for her safety.

"Yeah, way out of the way. Like disappear." She looked up at him. "I'll be back in a couple of minutes."

She returned with a bowl of soapy water and a sponge. She began scrubbing away the words scribbled on the wall. The toxic words disappeared fairly quickly. She turned and looked at Marc again. "I'm done. Let's go inside."

They sat in silence together on the sofa.

Finally Marc spoke. "If Cass is right in his speculation, then this guy is targeting you because he doesn't want to take a chance that you'll come in late and catch him in the act. He just wants you gone, out of the way. So he's trying to scare you, and he's using vile language to run you off."

"I'm not running."

Marc could hear the determination in her voice. ""I know you're not running. But we have to be sensible and smart about this. We want to catch him, but even more than that, we want you to be safe."

Angela looked at him. She had tears in her eyes.

Marc decided that it was time for him to take the lead. "Okay, here's what we're going to do. First, we'll go to one of the stores that sells the surveillance equipment and get what we need. There are a few stores that stay open late. Then we're going back to my place, and we'll spend the night there. You can sleep in my bed, and I'll sleep on the sofa. We'll get up really early, like three thirty a.m. tomorrow morning, go to your clinic, install the cameras, and be home about an hour later, before five a.m. Then you call in sick when the clinic opens. The shithead will think he's scared you off. But we'll be watching to see what he does next. Catch him in the act."

Angela brushed away her tears. "I'm causing you a lot of trouble."

Marc laughed derisively. "You're not even a tiny drop of trouble compared to some of the misery I saw when I was working."

"But..."

Marc cut her off. "Actually, trying to keep you safe makes me feel better about myself. I don't feel so useless."

"You're not useless."

"When I was in Sudan, I saw a young girl being raped by three men. She was maybe ten or twelve. Really young. When the last one got off her and walked away, she struggled to her feet. She stood there sobbing, blood dripping down between her legs. They really hurt her. I couldn't do a damn thing to stop them or to help her. They had me tied up with the barrel of a gun to my head. Useless."

Angela leaned against his chest, her arms around him. "Marc?"

"Sorry. I shouldn't have told you that."

"Stop apologizing or I'm going to get pissed off."

Marc looked at her. She was smiling at him. "You're so special," he said.

"You're the special one. Don't forget that. Okay. I'll go along with your plan. Let's go get the surveillance equipment first. But let me go get a few things to take with me. My toothbrush. A change of clothes. I'll be back in a minute."

Angela returned quickly carrying a small bag of personal items, and a second bag with her veterinarian medical equipment. "Let's go."

Marc drove them to a large store that carried electronic equipment. They found and purchased what they needed, and they were back at his apartment within the hour.

"This is working out well," Angela said. "But I can sleep on the sofa. You don't have to give up your bed."

"Will you stop resisting me about every little thing, please!" Marc smiled. "I am your host. It is my pleasure that you sleep in my bed. I'll even change the sheets for you. Now let's hit the sack because we have to get up really, really early."

"Don't worry about the sheets. Set the alarm, kiss me goodnight, and I'll see you in the morning."

Marc took her in his arms and kissed her. He knew the kisses were becoming more passionate, hungrier, but he couldn't stop himself. He loved kissing her, and he loved even more that she kissed him right back. He released her. "You are a ray of light."

Angela smiled. "Set the alarm, and I'll see you in the morning."

Marc set the radio for the local public radio station. He was awakened at three thirty a.m. by the sound of a BBC commentator updating him on what time it was in London. He groaned, forced himself off the sofa, went to pee, and then went to his bedroom. "Angela, wake up, lazy bones."

He blinked. She wasn't there. He turned around just as she threw her arms around him.

"I'm awake!"

"Oh god. Are you one of those weirdos who wake up cheerful every morning?" He rubbed his eyes.

Angela kissed him on his cheek. "Go get dressed, and I'll make us some coffee."

Marc threw on his clothes, went downstairs with Gwenny to give her a chance to pee, and when he returned, Angela thrust a cup of coffee in his hands. Gwenny went back to her crate.

They took their coffee with them in the car, along with the surveillance equipment and Marc's laptop computer. He parked about half a block away on a side street. They walked to the veterinary clinic, and Angela unlocked the back door. "I have the key to get in so the alarm system won't go off."

Angela directed him to the room where the medications were kept. She locked the door behind her and flipped on the overhead florescent lights. Marc noticed that the room had no windows. Good, he thought. The light isn't visible from outside the building.

Marc began inspecting the room. He pointed to a vent near the ceiling. "I can put the camera up there inside the vent, but I don't know how the air conditioning blowing on it all day will affect it. I could try it, but I think we need a better view anyway, a view of this counter top. Am I correct in assuming that vials of medication are on the shelves of this cabinet above the counter top?"

"Yes, exactly."

"What's in the cabinet on the other side of the room?"

"Stuff like paper towels, bandages, gauze, disposable surgical sheets. And on the bottom shelf are different kinds of surgical equipment, like different kinds of forceps, retractors, scissors, and the like. The vials of medications and sedatives are kept completely separate."

Marc climbed onto a chair and looked at the top of the cabinet with the surgical supplies and equipment. "It's a little bit recessed up here on top. I can put the camera up here and then put a lens on a short extension cable so that the lens peeks above the top of the cabinet. It will be just barely visible."

He started work immediately, and Angela helped by handing him tools. It just took a few minutes. He climbed back down, and opened his laptop. He clicked on some keys. Angela watched over his shoulder.

"Oh, look!" she said. "I can see the top of your head and the meds cabinet behind us."

"I'm going to move out of the way. You sit at the counter top and pretend you're getting something out of the cabinet." Angela nodded. She sat, then unlocked the cabinet and pulled out a vial of medicine.

"Perfect," Marc said. "I see everything."

"You really know what you're doing," Angela said.

"This is really easy," Marc waved his hand dismissively.

"Yeah, it's easy for you because you know what you're doing. I just hope with all my heart that we can catch this dude. I want to feel safe again."

"You will feel safe again. I'm going to make sure of that. Let's go home."

Thirty minutes later, they were back at Marc's apartment, and both he and Angela were falling asleep again.

* * *

A quick breakfast and two cups of coffee each meant that both were ready to face the day. Angela called her veterinary clinic. Marc heard her tell the receptionist that she wasn't feeling at all well, and she feared maybe she was coming down with something. She was sure she had a fever.

After she disconnected, Angela turned to Marc and said, "I don't like lying."

"In this case, you have to. If they are convinced you're sick, they won't expect you in for at least a couple of days, maybe a week. I hope we have this solved by then."

Angela's phone chimed. She looked at the phone and said to Marc, "This is a text from Cass. He says that no one who works for my veterinary clinic has a police record. However, Eric's brother, Braden, has been in and out of jail multiple times for dealing drugs."

Marc frowned. "Braden was the man with Eric on the surveillance camera here at Casa Pacifica."

"Yeah. So there's definitely a drug connection."

Marc nodded. "Maybe this will be easy. Let's check the camera." He opened the laptop, clicked on a few keys, and was disappointed to see a dark room.

"We have to wait until someone comes in and turns on the light," Angela explained.

"Well, I don't want to sit around all day watching my laptop screen. How about if we go take a look at some place new. Have you ever been to Summerhaven?"

"No," she said. "I'm not exactly sure what that is. It's something up the mountain." She pointed to the Santa Catalina Mountains just to the north of Tucson.

"Summerhaven is a little village high up on Mount Lemmon. We'll be surrounded by pine forests, and it will be a lot cooler than it is in Tucson this time of year. It's a tourist destination with shops and places to eat. There are a lot of hiking trails and places to camp nearby. And a short distance outside of Summerhaven, there's a ski resort, Mount Lemmon Ski Valley."

"Really? I've never been to a ski resort."

"It's the southern-most ski resort in America. But there's no snow now in late April. We can go skiing next winter."

"This sounds great!"

"So you want to go?"

"Yes!"

"There's one other thing you should know. My parents live in Summerhaven. We could go visit them. Maybe eat lunch. My mother loves to cook."

Marc immediately noticed that Angela had stopped smiling. She looked worried.

"What's wrong?" he asked.

"What if your parents don't like me?"

He frowned. "Why do you think they wouldn't like you?"

"What if white parents don't want their white son to bring home a black girl?"

"Don't be affected by what that asshole wrote on your friend's wall. My parents aren't racists. My dad is an animal lover. He has two dogs and three cats, some fish, two birds, and a snake in a glass tank container thingy. He'll try to take you off in the corner and have an hour-long conversation on some hot topic like doggy arthritis. He will love you."

Angela laughed. "I'll take my medical bag."

"My mother may be a problem, though." He couldn't help but tease her a little.

"Oh," Angela sighed, clearly disappointed.

"My mom is a cook, a very serious cook. She thinks that Americans don't know how to cook pasta. She says Americans make a god-awful mess of pasta, a sloppy, mushy mess. How's your pasta?"

Angela grinned. "I know all about that. I cook pasta *al dente*."

"*Al dente*? Very good. Then you'll pass the pasta test." He returned her grin.

"What about Gwenny?" she asked.

"Gwenny will go with us. This will be her chance to interact with my dad's dogs and cats."

"Good idea."

"Okay. I'll call my mom and tell her we're coming. She'll be relieved. I haven't been up there since I arrived home."

"Then you'll make her happy."

"There's one other thing. My real name isn't Marc. It's really Marco."

"Marco! Marco Tomassone. Oh, my god. That's so Italian, so sexy."

Marc laughed. "You know how to make a man feel good."

"Oh, sugar. You don't know," Angela said in a sultry, Southern voice. "There will come a time when I will make you feel really, really good."

Whoa! Marc thought to himself. Could that mean what he thought it meant? He hoped so! Wow!

They drove up the highway from Tucson to Summerhaven, enjoying all the twists and turns and fabulous views along the way. "Note as we climb, we'll go through different biomes. The desert floor is dry and hot. As we climb, we'll see more saguaros, then trees start to appear. Mesquite and palo verde mostly. Then even higher, we'll go into the pine forests," Marc explained.

"Fascinating. I love this," she responded.

"Tell me about your family and whatever in New Orleans." Marc kept his eyes on the road.

"Whatever?" Angela laughed.

"I don't know what I mean. I just want to know you better."

"I had a very easy childhood. My parents had good incomes so we never had poverty problems. My dad was an elementary school principal, and my mom taught high school history. Our house was an older home on a large lot, nearly a quarter of an acre. We had a big vegetable garden and several pets. My pets, my dogs and cats, convinced me to become a veterinarian."

"Siblings?"

"No siblings. My mom had me, and she couldn't have any more babies. I have lots of cousins, though. How about you?"

"I have two older sisters. One got a great job in Phoenix, met this guy there, married him and stayed in Phoenix, actually Mesa. No kids yet, but they are talking about it. The other sister went to Italy on a trip to see our family, met this Italian dude, married him and stayed in Italy. She has two kids already. I have a lot of cousins, too. In Italy."

"Why did your parents come to Tucson?"

"My dad is a scholar. He was writing a book about Father Kino, the Spanish padre who established the San Xavier del Bac mission. Except that Father Kino wasn't really Spanish. He was an Italian priest. Don't get my dad started on this or else he'll talk your ear off. Anyway, the University of Arizona invited him first as a visiting scholar, and he ended up being appointed a professor. My sisters and I were born and grew up here."

"Did you speak Italian at home?"

"Yes. And we still do unless I bring home a beautiful girl from New Orleans who doesn't know a word of Italian."

"I know Italian!"

"Okay. Let's hear it."

"Pizza. Lasagna. Pasta. Spaghetti."

Marc laughed. "That will do. But we're supposed to be talking about you. What do your parents think about you living in Arizona?"

Angela frowned. "When I was in vet school, my dad died suddenly of a heart attack. Then my mom was diagnosed with breast cancer. After I graduated, I got a job in the New Orleans area, and I moved in with my mom and took care of her until she passed."

"I'm sorry to hear that."

"After she died, I was sad a lot, and I needed to try something new. Try living a new way. I'd already done some volunteer gigs, and I decided to do some more. As I mentioned, one of the gigs was here in Arizona traveling around to the Native reservations. I loved Tucson so I started looking for a job here. That's how I ended up here."

Marc nodded.

"I have something else to tell you," Angela said. "I was married."

Marc's eyebrows went up. "But you're not married now?"

"No. In my last year of vet school, I came home one day and found my husband in bed with a strange woman. *My* bed! The neighbors told me later that she wasn't the first. He'd been bringing women home for months. I divorced him. That's another reason why I wanted to leave New Orleans and move to Tucson. You're not married, are you?"

Marc shook his head no. "I had a serious girlfriend, but she dumped me. She said I wasn't ambitious enough. She told me that she wanted to live an affluent life, and I was unlikely to make that happen for her. She was very frank."

"Good riddance," Angela said emphatically. "For both you and me."

By now, they had arrived at the pine forests. Marc drove into the village of Summerhaven, gave Angela a quick look at the town, then he went right onto a narrow road that led past several homes. He turned into the driveway of one of the homes.

Only a minute later, an older woman with white hair came out of the house and waved. She was grinning ear to ear. "*Mio caro figlio!*" she called out.

"What's she saying?" Angela asked.

"'*Mi caro figlio*' means 'my dear son.'"

Angela and Marc got out of the car. By that time, Marc's mother had him in a hug, had kissed him on both cheeks and was chattering in Italian.

"Mamma, this is Angela. Angela, this is my mother, Francesca."

Marc's mother hugged Angela and kissed her both cheeks. "*Benvenuta. Che bella*! *Che bella*!" she said.

"What's she saying?" Angela asked.

"She says 'welcome' and she thinks you are beautiful. '*Bella*' is 'beautiful.'"

"Oh!" Angela was grinning now.

"Mamma, *parla l'inglese*! Speak English!"

Marc's father had appeared now. He was accompanied by three dogs, a black Lab, a Golden Retriever, and a tan-and-white pit bull mix. Angela could see the cats sitting on the porch watching them. The house was a classic Summerhaven cabin, wood inside and out. Angela could see a rock chimney rising from the roof.

"Papa, this is Angela. My dad, Antonio Tomassone."

Later Angela would tell Marc that, except for white hair and wrinkles, she thought Marc and his dad looked remarkably alike. Handsome. Very handsome.

Angela received kisses on both cheeks from Marc's dad. "*Benvenuta*! Welcome."

"Papa, I see you have a new dog. We have a dog, too." Marc looked at both his parents and rattled off something in Italian. He turned to Angela. "I'm explaining about Gwenny."

Angela had the slip leash on Gwenny now and tried to draw her out, but the dog didn't want to leave the back-seat of the car. She was looking at the three dogs who were looking at her. Their tails wagging, but Gwenny was trembling in fear.

Antonio stepped forward and took the leash. He bent down and began to stroke Gwenny and speak to her in a soft voice. "*Cara mia, non ai paura.*"

"He's telling Gwenny that's she's dear to him, and there's no need to be afraid."

Marc's dad managed to convince Gwenny to come out of the car. He took her to meet the other dogs. They quickly surrounded her, tails wagging, sniffed her, and then walked away. Gwenny looked far less terrified now.

"That went well," Marc said.

"*Vieni! Vieni con me!*" Marc's mom called out. Come! Come with me!

Marc took Angela's hand. "Let's go inside."

Once inside, Marc said to Angela, "I'm going to introduce you, tell them about how you are a veterinarian, you came from New Orleans, and all that. I'm going to say it in Italian so it will go faster. My mom doesn't speak English as well as my dad." He turned to his parents and told them all about Angela.

Antonio turned to Angela and said, "Excellent. Excellent. I wonder if I could talk to you about my Lab's hip joints? She is having problems. I think maybe it's arthritis."

Marc chuckled and turned to Angela. "Told you so."

"Yes, of course, Mr. Tomassone. I'll go get my bag. I can examine all your dogs. And your cats, too. My pleasure."

Antonio Tomassone was grinning now. He gathered the dogs at a sofa near a large window in the living room, and Angela left briefly to collect her medical bag. She returned quickly, Gwenny with her, and she joined Marc's dad. By that time, Marc's mother had dragged her son into her kitchen.

"Marco, *mi caro figlio*," she began. Then a long string of questions followed. Where did you meet Angela? Is she really a veterinarian? Is she a good woman? Do you love her? Are you going to marry her? How many children will you have? Does she know how to cook?

Marc was laughing now. "Mamma, she knows how to properly cook pasta. *Al dente!*"

"*Che miracolo!*" What a miracle! She hugged him again, smiling.

Marc looked over and saw Angela with her stethoscope around her neck. She had a cat on her lap. An hour or so later, Angela had examined all of the Tomassone dogs and cats. She gave Marc's dad a prescription for the Lab, now officially diagnosed as arthritic. She also gave him a bottle of pills to prevent heart worms in both dogs and cats, with a prescription to get more when the supply ran out.

Meanwhile, Marc's mother had created a feast. She told him to fetch Angela and his dad. Time to eat. They all sat at the table, but before they began, Francesca said a brief prayer in Italian, and crossed herself. She began filling the wine glasses. Then she sat down and said firmly, "*Mangiamo! Mangiamo!*"

Marc heard Angela whisper to herself, "*Mangiamo.*"

"That means, 'let's eat.'"

"I'm going to remember that," she smiled.

The time passed quickly and pleasantly. The meal included delicious traditional Italian dishes, and Francesca was enthusiastically praised for her cooking. Their dinner ended with a dessert dish of cannoli. Francesca explained, "We're not Sicilian. We're northern Italian, but Americans like cannoli."

Marc laughed to himself. His mother liked cannoli, too. Finally, when they couldn't eat any more, he said, "We have to go home now. I'd like to return to Tucson before dark."

Hugs and goodbyes all around came next. Marc and Angela drove away, waving at Antonio and Francesca who were standing in their driveway, waving and blowing kisses. Gwenny nodded off in the backseat.

Marc and Angela never noticed the car that had followed them up the mountain to Summerhaven, nor did they notice the person in the car who had taken a photo of Antonio and Francesca's home when the family was inside, nor did they notice the same car that followed them all the way back to the Iron Horse neighborhood.

8 Surprises

"Did you know you wave your hands a lot when you talk, especially when you speak Italian?" Angela smiled at him.

Marc was pulling his car into its parking place behind Casa Pacifica Apartments. "Italians can't talk without their hands waving. It's genetic." He grinned and wiggled his eyebrows. He turned off the car's engine.

Angela laughed. "I think it's learned behavior, not genetic. Your parents do the same. It's really cute."

"Cute?" Marc shook his head and sighed. "Cute? Not my idea of the best way to be viewed by a beautiful woman."

"Okay, I'll admit. Cute, handsome, sexy as hell, a real hottie. That all describes you." She laughed again.

"That's better."

"Your mother said a particular word several times."

"What? Pasta?" He smiled at her.

"No. The word was '*compleanno*.'"

Marc said nothing. He looked away.

"Marco, Marco, Marco," she grinned. "Your face is turning red. What does that word mean?"

He sighed. "Birthday."

"Is today your birthday? Oh, goodness. Why didn't you tell me?"

"Not today. Next Sunday."

"And she wants you to return to their place for your birthday? I'm going to get you a birthday gift."

"My mother makes a fuss over me."

"Of course, she does. I'm going to learn Italian. And talk with my hands to your parents." She held up her hands and wiggled her fingers again.

"What shall we eat for supper?"

"You're trying to change the subject. Anyway, I'll never eat again. I'm stuffed."

"Yeah, me, too. We'll let Gwenny eat for us. She did great today, don't you think?"

"Yes, I think she's well on the way to overcoming her anxiety."

They went up to Marc's apartment, and he fed Gwenny some kibble and filled her water bowl.

"It's a good thing that we're not hungry. I don't have any fresh food. How about a glass of wine?"

"Sure. We can go walk to the market later this evening and get some groceries. I'll cook for you. And then I'll say, '*Mangiamo!*'"

"Don't forget to wave your hands when you say that."

"I will." Angela waved her hands in the air again. "I'm practicing."

Marc laughed. "*Molto bene.* That means 'very good.'"

They sat down together on the sofa. Marc leaned back, crossed his legs at his ankles and sighed. "It's good to be home."

Angela nodded. "Funny thing. I feel at home for the first time since I came to Tucson."

They fell silent for a few minutes.

Marc was looking straight ahead, not at Angela. He took a sip of wine and said, "I wish I could be one of your dogs. I mean the ones you take care of."

Angela sat her glass down. "Why?"

He put his wine glass down, too. "Because you stroke the dog's head…"

Angela moved closer to him. She leaned into him and began stroking his dark curls.

"And you nuzzle against the dog, and you kiss him."

Angela did just that. The kiss was long and sweet.

"And you tell him that he's a good boy."

Angela smiled. "You *are* a good boy."

"Am I? I'm not useless?"

"Don't say that again. You are not useless. You are a good boy. You are a very good boy, and you deserve a treat."

"A treat?"

Angela removed her arm from his shoulder and began to unbutton her blouse. Marc's eyes widened. She had on a see-through, push-up bra. He couldn't stop looking. So beautiful.

"Let's go lie down on your bed, and I'll give you a treat," she said.

Marc found that he couldn't talk. He took her hand and followed Angela to his bed.

A little more than an hour later, they both woke up at the same time.

"That was a surprise," Marc said as he held Angela close. "That was a surprise and the very best treat of my life."

"Continue being good, and you'll get more treats. And I must add, you are very, very good at what you do." She stroked his chest.

Marc kissed her. He actually felt happy, much to his surprise. He hadn't felt happy in a long, long time.

* * *

"Enough of this naughty stuff," Angela chuckled. "You know I won't be able to resist you. You are a magnificent lover, Marco Tomassone. *Molto bene.* So how about if we take a look at the surveillance camera's video and see if anything interesting has happened at the vet clinic today?"

Marc retrieved his laptop, and they sat together to see what the video had recorded. For most of the day, the veterinarians and their assistants went in and out of the meds room. Marc fast forwarded through hours of that. Then, in the late afternoon, the traffic into the meds room slowed, then stopped all together. The room was dark.

"Maybe we'll see some action soon," Marc said. "It's almost seven in the evening now."

Much to their surprise, both Dr. Ted Wilden, the owner of the veterinary practice, and Dr. Freddy Varo, the veterinarian most recently hired, came into the room at the same time. Wilden closed and locked the door behind him. Then he and Dr. Varo fell into an intense embrace, kissing each other and touching each other all over. Buttons and zippers were being unfastened, and items of clothing were being removed.

Angela gasped. "Oh, my god. What are they doing?"

Marc was both embarrassed and amused. "Looks like they are having sex with each other."

Angela had covered her face. She was giggling uncontrollably. "I can't believe it." She looked back at the screen. "Oh, my god. We shouldn't be watching this, but I can't stop watching." She giggled. "I'm so embarrassed." She turned to Marc. "I don't know what to say."

"Me neither. This is totally unexpected."

"So you've never done this before?"

"With a guy? No! I like girls. I've always liked girls."

"This is like a porn show."

"Yeah, and it's sort of becoming boring like most porn shows."

"I thought men liked porn."

"Not all men are alike, Angela. To me, sex for sex's sake is kind of like scratching a bad itch because the itch is driving you crazy. You know what I mean? Relief. Nothing more. I've had plenty of sex like that, especially when I was a teen and in my early twenties. For me, sex is so very much better if it's making love with someone you really care about. Making love. Like we did earlier today. That's the best."

"You really are special," Angela said. She leaned toward him and kissed him on his cheek.

"Look. We did not expect to see this at all. I mean two guys getting it on. And, frankly, I think we can just go right past this. We can just forget we saw this, and focus instead on the drug problem," he said.

"I agree. So fast forward, and let's see what happens next."

Ted and Freddy were in the meds room no more than half an hour. Time passed. All was quiet. Now it was nearly nine p.m. Eric and Brandon entered the room and locked it behind them.

"That's Braden, Eric's brother," Marc said. "He's not supposed to be there."

Angela and Marc sat holding hands with each other, mesmerized at what came next. Eric took several vials from the shelf and methodically began using a needle and syringe to remove some of the contents from each bottle. He transferred the drug contents to empty vials. Braden wrote something on paper labels, then stuck the labels on several bottles that now contained the drug hydromorphone. They were doing exactly what Cass Cosay had described.

"These two working together makes this all go faster," Marc said.

"And probably Braden is the one who will sell the opioid hydromorphone," Angela added. She turned to Marc. "I need to get some of those altered vials and have them tested so I can prove to Ted that someone is altering the contents."

"Yes, but let's wait another day. I want to make sure no one is following you. You're supposed to be sick so let's give it another day."

Suddenly both men turned their heads sharply toward the door. There was the faint sound of knocking and an even fainter sound of a voice.

"Now who could that be?" Marc was frowning.

Braden opened the door, and a woman walked in. She closed the door behind her and locked it. Marc noticed that she was probably mid-forties in age, had stylish, short-cut hair, expensive clothing, and a lot of jewelry. Earrings, several bracelets and rings, and at least two necklaces adorned the woman who was now frowning at the two men.

Angela gasped. "Oh, for god's sake. What's she doing there?"

"You know this woman?"

"Yeah, Phoebe is Ted's wife."

"Your boss, Ted? The head of the clinic?"

Angela nodded.

"Let's listen to the conversation," Marc said.

"You followed her?" Phoebe was talking to Braden.

"Yes. I took photos. They visited an old couple up the mountains in Summerhaven."

Phoebe looked at Eric. "And you. Keeping busy?" Her laugh was brief and insincere.

"You won't tell anybody, will you?" Eric asked.

"Not if you follow my instructions." Phoebe turned back to Braden. "And now I want you to complete our little arrangement." She handed Braden an envelope stuffed with something. "It's time to get rid of her. Here's the payoff."

Braden took a step back. "Look. Drug dealing is one thing, but…" He turned to Eric. "What will happen to Eric? I don't want us both to spend the rest of our lives in jail."

"Too late to be thinking about that now," Phoebe said harshly. "With your record, if I turn you in for drug dealing, you will be a resident of the state prison for many, many years. And, you, too, Eric."

Eric looked at his brother. Braden's frown had deepened. He said nothing.

"All right. I'll be keeping track of this. I expect a resolution soon." She turned, unlocked the door, and walked out.

"Shit," muttered Braden. "Eric, finish that bottle, and let's get the hell out of here."

Eric followed Braden's instructions. They left the meds room only a few minutes later.

Marc looked at Angela. Her eyes were filled with tears. He reached out and took her hand.

"I don't know what to do," she said.

Marc was quiet. Finally, he said, "Yeah. I'm not happy that we were being followed, and we didn't even notice. And my parents. That's so unacceptable. Let's go talk to Logan. I'd like to run this by him, and see if he comes to the same conclusion as I have."

"What's your conclusion?"

"You and I are in trouble."

Tears began to roll down her face.

"Angela, listen to me. I'm going to keep you safe. We'll find a way out of this."

"I don't know what to do."

"Come on. Let's go see Logan."

* * *

Logan answered the door, a dish towel in his hands. His smile faded when he saw Angela and Marc's faces. "Something wrong?"

"Can we talk to you for a few minutes?"

Logan turned back and said, "Zoey, I'll be gone a few minutes. Charlie, ask Zoey if she needs any help with the dishes."

The three went to sit in the side yard in their favorite lawn chairs. Marc updated Logan on what was happening. He included the sexual encounter they'd witnessed between the two male vets. Then he went into detail about the conversation that Phoebe had with Braden and Eric.

"So this woman Phoebe knows all about these guys and their drug business?"

"Yes," Marc said. "I think she's blackmailing them about the drug business. She expects them to do her bidding or she'll tell all. Worse, she's paying one of them, the tall one we saw in the surveillance video here at our apartments. She's paying him to do harm to someone." He glanced over at Angela. Tears were falling again. "Logan, I'm fearful that it's Angela she's after."

Logan nodded. "Yes. The elder brother followed you to Summerhaven. That indicates that he's the one who is keeping track of Angela."

"That's bad. I don't want my parents involved." Marc shook his head no.

Logan turned to Angela. "Why you? Have you had some kind of conflict with her?"

"No. I've barely spoken to her."

Marc spoke up. "Remember you telling me about how you witnessed them have a shouting match? They were arguing because she thought her husband was having an affair?"

Angela nodded, "She yelled at him to tell her who 'she' was." She paused. "Oh, that's it. Phoebe said 'she.' She thinks I'm the one who's having an affair with Ted."

"And she knows nothing about his gay lover," Logan added.

"Right," Marc said. "No telling what she'll do if she finds out about the other vet."

Logan added, "Interesting thing. Some people don't take a gay interaction very seriously, and they just dismiss it. They find out a spouse is doing it with a same-sex person, and they just look the other way, like they don't take gay sex seriously. To them it's not real sex. Other people get furious and come out guns blazing. They take it very seriously as an outrageous form of infidelity. So Phoebe's reaction to finding the truth is unpredictable."

"We can't take a chance on how she reacts to anything. I want to keep Angela safe."

"I'm going back to my apartment and call my contact at the Tucson Police Department, Detective Julio Alvarez," Logan said. "I'll tell him everything, and ask how best to handle this."

"What do you think we should do now?" Marc asked.

"Better keep a low profile. I'll ask Alvarez about that, too. Back in a minute." Logan returned to his apartment.

Angela looked at Marc. "I'm so sorry. This is so unfair. I really don't want to drag you into this mess. Maybe I should pack my bags and leave Tucson."

Marc shook his head. "No way." He fell quiet for a few minutes, then said, "Hey! I know how to distract you. Want to know what my mom asked me about you when she was rattling on in the kitchen?"

"What did she say about me? Stay away from that woman. She's nothing but trouble."

"No. She said you are sweet and beautiful and kind. She wants to know if we're getting married and how many children are we going to have." He paused. Good grief. Why the hell was he telling her that? Maybe he should slow down. Or not. Whatever.

"Did she say that? My mom liked to make plans for me, too."

Marc nodded.

"Here's what I think. You and I should come up with our own plan. We'll go at our own pace, and we'll do what's right for us." Angela touched his hand.

"Together? Our own pace?"

"Yes." A soft smile appeared on her lips. "And if your mom mentions this again, you can tell her that I've fallen madly in love with her son. The rest of it is up to him."

Oh, wow. He hadn't expected that. Okay. Time to get real. "Good. I love you, too, although it sounds better in Italian. *Ti amo*, Angela, *ti amo*. We'll work out the details as we go along. At our own pace."

"Yes, let's go with the flow."

Marc smiled. "But be assured that before we make any babies, we have to practice a lot."

"Practice what?" She was smiling now.

"You know where babies come from, don't you?" He squeezed her hand.

"I think so. It involves a lot of Marco treats."

"Correct. Many, many treats."

"Because you're a good boy. Oh, so good. You make *me* feel very, very good when I give you a treat."

Marc grinned just as Logan reappeared.

"Okay. I talked to Alvarez. He's coming over here at nine in the morning so expect a knock on your door around then. He's also going to have a patrol car drive by every now and then this evening. Marc, I gave him your phone number. He'll probably text before he comes."

Marc and Angela stood up. "Thank you so much, Logan."

"Stay safe, you two." He turned to go. "If you need anything, Zoey and I will get it for you. You're invited to come to breakfast tomorrow morning, too."

"We will," Marc said. "Thank you." He took Angela's hand, and they returned to his apartment.

9 CONFRONTATION

"What shall we do now?" Marc asked when they returned to his apartment. "I don't want to go outside. Braden may be waiting for us."

"I have an idea. I'd like to see your photographs." Angela took his hand.

Marc frowned and shook his head. "You don't want to see all that. Blood and misery, I mean."

"I don't mean your war photos. I want to see photos from before. I mean before you went into those war zones."

"Are you sure? It's just a bunch of silly, arty stuff."

"I like arty stuff." She leaned in and kissed him. "Please."

He sighed. "Okay. But I think you'll be disappointed."

"Of course you think that. You've been in a dark state since you came home. You're suffering from a weariness of spirit, a melancholy caused by the awful things you saw. I'm going to do my best to help you get past all that, and get back to your true self."

"Does this mean more Marco treats?" He smiled.

"Yes, but even more than that. You'll see. So go get your photos, and I'll decide if they are silly, arty stuff. I actually know a fair amount about art. I'm from New Orleans, you know. Art, music, and food. New Orleans."

Marc went to a chest in his bedroom, and he came back with several heavy manila folders. He sat them on the dining room table. Angela was already there, waiting. She began methodically going through the folders. After the third folder, she was frowning and shaking her head.

Rats, Marc said to himself. She hates my photos. She thinks they're garbage. "That bad, huh?" he said.

Angela looked at him. "Sorry to say this, but you are confused."

"What? What do you mean?"

"Your photos are gorgeous. Definitely fine art. These color photos of the mountains and the saguaro are beyond beautiful. The sunsets are breathtaking."

Why did he have a sudden feeling of...what? Uncertainty? Relief? Happiness? "That one is Baboquivari Peak." He pointed to the photo she was holding.

"And these." She pointed to a file with image after image of wild horses running. "Stunning."

"I took those in the Salt River Valley north of here."

"The black-and-white photos are just as good. Where did you take these ocean scenes?"

"The Gulf of California, also known as the Sea of Cortez. That's the body of water between the main part of Mexico and Baja California."

"Okay. I know what you mean. I've read that there's an endangered porpoise living there."

"Yeah, it's called a vaquita. There are only a few left in the northern Sea of Cortez. We can go there sometime if you want. It's not far from Tucson."

"Yes, I'd like to see it. For sure."

"So if you like my photos, why do you think I'm confused?"

"Because you don't recognize your artistry. You devalue your work, and you devalue yourself. It's part of your weariness of spirit. But don't worry. I'm going to help you. You're my good boy."

Marc laughed. "This sounds like more love making. Count me in."

She rolled her eyes. "Yeah, but it's more than that. Before this is all over, you'll be showing in galleries and selling your artwork like hotcakes. Just you wait and see." She nodded firmly. "You'll have way more confidence in yourself then. I'm going to help you."

"What can I do for you?"

"You've already done a lot," Angela said seriously. "I love Tucson, but I didn't know how lonely I was until you came along. I love being with you. I love your Casa Pacifica family. I love your Summerhaven family. I love your dog. And I love you."

"Does this mean more Marco treats?"

"Sure. How about now?" She smiled at him.

He laughed and grabbed her hand. "Let's go to my bedroom, Dr. Brooks."

* * *

The next morning, Marc and Angela showered together. "We have to shower together to save water," Marc said seriously but his lips were twitching in an attempt to not laugh. "We live in a desert, you know?"

Angela laughed and kissed him. "Then stop what you're doing to me, or we'll be in here for a long time!"

"Yeah, you're right. I need to take Gwenny out, too. And we've been invited to breakfast."

Out of the shower and dressed, Marc leashed Gwenny. "Stay here and keep the door locked."

"I will," Angela said solemnly.

Marc took Gwenny out to the street in front of the Casa Pacifica apartments. While Gwenny did her business, Marc looked up and down the street. All was quiet.

The nearest car was almost a block away. He returned to the apartment and unlocked the door with his key. Gwenny found her bowl full of kibble right away, thanks to Angela. The two of them sipped coffee as Gwenny ate her breakfast.

"Marc, while you were downstairs with Gwenny, I called my friend Cynthia. I told you already about how I've been house sitting for her. She told me that she's on her way home now. I told her what was going on here, and why I left her house. I expressed concern about her safety, but she told me not to worry. Her boyfriend is with her. I've met him. He's a big guy, a former linebacker with some pro football team. I'm pretty sure he can keep her safe from a weenie like Eric."

"Good. When this all over, we'll go get the rest of your stuff. But for now, it's time to go eat breakfast," Marc said. Gwenny went with them, going down the stairs like a pro, as if the dog had never been afraid of anything.

When they arrived at Logan's door, Marc knocked. Charlie flung the door open, squealed "Gwenny!" and then he ran away, giggling the entire time. Gwenny went after him, tail wagging. She did a play bow, then tried to lick Charlie's face. Charlie jumped up with a ball in his hand. He threw the ball across the room. "Fetch!" he called out. Gwenny went after the ball, picked it up in her mouth, and brought it right back to Charlie. "Oh, such a good girl, Gwenny. You're so smart." He put the ball down, ran to the other side of the room. Gwenny followed him. Charlie pointed to the ball and again called, "Fetch!" Gwenny's eyes went to where Charlie pointed. She quickly retrieved the ball and brought it to Charlie. This time, the dog was given a dog biscuit as a reward.

"Okay, Charlie, enough of that," Logan said. "It's time for breakfast. Go wash your hands."

Zoey came out of the kitchen holding a hot skillet with oven mittens. "Logan made us one of his famous frittatas. Want some coffee or orange juice?"

They all sat together, eating, and chatting. Marc swung back and forth between the pleasure of being at home with friends as well as being with Angela, versus the concern and worry he had about keeping her safe.

"What's everyone doing today?" Marc asked. He wanted to know who would be in the building when the police detective showed up.

"I'm going to a soccer team meeting and make plans for our next season," Zoey said, "but not until this afternoon."

"Li is at work early for a special breakfast event for some local business group. Xochi is moving her stuff in box-by-box. I don't expect to see her again until this afternoon. I have to go to the university later this morning and start cleaning out my office. My teaching gig will be over soon."

"Think you'll miss teaching?" Marc asked.

"I've applied for a job at Pima Community College. Maybe I won't have to miss it."

Marc turned to Charlie. "What are you doing today?"

"I'm not going to school!"

"No?" Marc grinned. "Are you on strike?"

Charlie frowned. "What's a strike?"

Marc looked over at Logan. "Want to explain?"

"A strike is when you are not happy about something, you protest it, and then you go on strike and refuse to work or cooperate with what's going on. Ask Frida about strikes sometime because she knows all about strikes. She can show you some photos."

"Okay, I'll ask her," Charlie said. He turned to Marc. "Zoey and I are going to watch birds this morning. What are you and Angela going to do?"

Marc hesitated. He didn't know if he should tell Charlie about a police detective coming to see them.

Angela smiled and said, "We're getting together with a friend of your dad's. Probably we'll drink some coffee or tea."

"That's nice. Can I play with Gwenny now?" Charlie was already looking over his shoulder at Gwenny lying on the rug.

"Sure." Marc was relieved.

"Thanks so much for breakfast. I hope we get things resolved quickly," Angela smiled. She and Marc were back in his apartment before nine a.m.

Detective Alvarez arrived right on time. He introduced himself, shook hands with both Marc and Angela, and said, "Busy day for me today so let's get started. Logan gave me an overview of what the problem is." He looked at Angela. "I understand that one of your veterinary clinic's employees appears to be siphoning off and stealing an opioid drug."

"That's correct, Angela said. "Marc is going to show you a video, and you can see for yourself what he's been doing."

Marc went to get his laptop, and all three sat at the dining table.

"Before we start, Detective Alvarez," Angela said, "I'd like to mention that there is some sensitive material in this video that has nothing to do with the drug theft. I very much hope that this can be kept private."

Alvarez nodded. "Let's see."

"The sensitive material will be the first thing we see," Marc explained. "The drug stuff comes later." He started the video.

Not long after, Alvarez witnessed the two male veterinarians deep into an intense sexual encounter. Alvarez laughed. "*Ai yi yi. Dios mio!*" He looked at Angela. "Who are these dudes?"

She pointed to the monitor. "That's Ted Wilden, the owner of the veterinarian clinic and head veterinarian. The other guy is Freddy Varo. He's a veterinarian, too." She looked at Alvarez. "You see what I mean? If this gets out, it could humiliate them both, and ruin Ted's vet practice. Put him out of business, I mean. I consider this private. It has nothing to do with the drug problem."

"Okay. I'll have to talk to my chief and probably the District Attorney about how to handle this. But looks like you're correct. This has nothing to do with the drug siphoning."

Marc fast-forwarded to the next live scene, Eric siphoning the opioid drug with help from his brother Braden. Detective Alvarez nodded. "We'll need to get samples so we can prove that some of the contents were altered and weakened."

By now, they were to the part of the video where the woman showed up. Marc paused the video.

"This is Phoebe Wilden," Angela said. "She's Ted Wilden's wife." Angela told Alvarez about hearing Ted and Phoebe's argument, and her demand to know with whom he was having an affair. "Phoebe thinks Ted's lover is a woman. We think she doesn't know about his gay lover."

"Listen carefully to their conversation," Marc said. He turned the speaker to a higher volume.

Alvarez stared intently at the video. When the episode was over, Alvarez sat back in his chair and said, "Very interesting. Looks like this woman, Phoebe Wilden, is blackmailing these guys. She found out about their drug activities, and now she's demanding that they commit an illegal act for her. I bet there's cash in that envelope which will make them killers-for-hire." He shook his head. "I'm sorry, Dr. Brooks. It does indeed look like she wants him to eliminate you."

Tears appeared in Angela's eyes.

"I'm not going to let that happen. If I have to take her away to Australia or Brazil or to the moon or wherever, I'm not going to let anyone hurt her," Marc said vehemently. He could feel his face getting hot.

"Okay. I think we can keep Dr. Brooks under wraps so no one will know where she is. The FBI has a safe house here. And if it's not available, we can take you to one of the women's shelters. Those shelters frequently have a problem with abusive husbands trying to break in and snatch their wives back again so very often the shelters have good security. Will you agree to that?"

"Yes, I can do that," Angela said.

"Also I'm going to put out an all-points-bulletin, an APB, on these two brothers. Eric will probably be easy to find, but no telling where Braden is. We'll bring him in, I'm sure."

"What can I do?" Marc asked.

"I need a copy of this video to start." Alvarez hesitated. "However, I'm going suggest that you archive this original. Then make me a copy without the sex scene, which I agree is not directly relevant to this case. We know that Wilden's wife suspected an affair, but she clearly thought that you are the guilty party, Dr. Brooks. So yes, archive the original and put an edited copy on a flash drive for me to take with me today. And we can keep this to ourselves."

Angela nodded. She whispered, "Thank you."

"If anyone figures out you've turned in an edited version," Marc added, "I'll take the heat on that, not you, Detective."

Alvarez nodded. "I'll need info about your surveillance project. I'm not sure how the prosecutor will handle that so we need as much info as possible. And I'll be going to the clinic this morning to get samples of those vials that have been altered. I may have to take quite a few so I can discover which ones are bad and how many there are. I'd also like to see that surveillance video that Logan Reid has of this apartment building. I'll check with him later about that. Also, Mr. Tomassone, stay in touch with your parents and make sure they are okay. I doubt these guys will bother them since Dr. Brooks is here in town, but it's a good idea to check on them."

Marc nodded. "What do we do next?"

"I'm going to call the FBI about the safe house first, then call for a TPD patrol car to come to this street, maybe park down the street, and watch to see if these guys show up looking for you, Dr. Brooks. You can come with me, and I'll take you directly to the safe house or one of the women's shelters if the safe house isn't available. Pack a few things to take with you. I'll go down first to my car. It's out in the front on the street. You can follow me in five minutes." Alvarez left Marc's apartment and headed downstairs.

Angela was close to sobs now. "Marc, I can't stay here, and you can't go with me. I'll miss you. I'll miss you terribly."

Marc held her in his arms. He felt that melancholia overcome him again. Then a sudden surge of resolve overcame the melancholia. "I meant it, my love. You will be safe, and you and I will be together again soon. I promise. Now go pack your bag and get your toothbrush and all that other girl stuff you left in my bathroom. I'll make a copy of the video now."

A few minutes later, Angela, Marc, and Gwenny went down the stairs and out the front door of Casa Pacifica apartments. They could see Alvarez standing next to his car and talking on his phone. Marc heard something behind him. Logan was coming out of the front door carrying a briefcase.

"I'm just now heading off to the university," Logan explained. The three of them started walking toward Alvarez.

Suddenly a woman appeared from the side yard. Phoebe! She'd been hiding behind a large creosote bush that was almost five feet tall, and no one had noticed her. She yelled out, "Stop!" In her hand, she held a gun that was pointed directly at them. She moved forward to stand at the foot of the entrance stairs.

"Phoebe!" Angela gasped.

Marc pulled Angela behind him.

"Angela, you bitch! I know what you've been doing with my husband. I'm going to make you pay." Phoebe looked at Marc. "Give her to me." She gestured with the gun toward Angela. "Get over here!"

At just that instant, the front door of Casa Pacifica flew open, and Charlie came running out at top speed carrying a backpack. At the same time, he called out, "Daddy, you forgot your backpack!" Then Charlie lost his footing and tripped. He tumbled down the stairs directly into Phoebe Wilden. She fell backwards, screeching.

Charlie's impact into Phoebe caused the gun in her hand to go flying as she tumbled backwards. It was a small gun, a Beretta pistol. The gun went up and away in an arc toward the street where it landed with a sharp metallic sound as it scraped against the concrete sidewalk. Phoebe began crawling on her knees toward the gun, yelling the entire time.

Charlie had already jumped to his feet, and he went running to his dad. Logan was running, too, and he met Charlie halfway.

Marc slipped the leash over Gwenny's head, and at the same time, he said to Charlie, "Tell Gwenny to fetch the gun."

Charlie called out loudly, "Fetch, Gwenny!" He pointed to the gun.

Gwenny the greyhound, the former racing dog who had spent most of her life in a cage, jumped into action. Her sleek body and long legs covered the space between Charlie and the gun in about three seconds. She zipped past Phoebe who was still screaming and crying now. Gwenny picked up the gun by its grip, and, trotting proudly, she brought it right back to Charlie. Logan reached down and took the gun. He sighed in relief, and then he handed the gun to Marc.

Charlie gave Gwenny a hug. "Good doggie! I love you, Gwenny."

Alvarez appeared now. He came running straight for Phoebe. He jerked her to her feet and pulled her arms behind her back. "I saw everything," he said roughly to Phoebe. Handcuffs came next. Just then, a Tucson Police Department patrol car pulled up, and two cops got out.

Logan could hear Alvarez informing Phoebe that she was under arrest. Miranda Rights came next. Logan heard Alvarez say, "You have a right to remain silent. Anything you say…" Alvarez turned away and began walking Phoebe Wilden toward the police patrol car. He finished the Miranda Rights and handed her over to the two cops. He turned back to Marc and gestured toward the gun. Marc handed it to him.

"Okay," Alvarez said. "You folks always have such exciting things happening here." He chuckled.

"Too much excitement." Logan frowned.

Marc handed the flash drive with the surveillance video on it to Alvarez.

"And here's something interesting," Alvarez added. "I called in that APB for Braden Carlson right after I left your apartment. It seems that one of our patrolmen stopped him for speeding this morning. Fifty-five in a thirty mile-per-hour zone. Just as the patrolman was writing out the ticket, he heard the APB on his patrol car radio. He arrested Braden Carlson on the spot, and Tucson Police Department is currently holding him in a cell. I'll be contacting you all soon for a formal statement. We'll be going to the vet clinic this morning and arrest Eric Carlson."

Alvarez waved goodbye and returned to his car.

Logan leaned down to Charlie. "Are you hurt, Charlie?"

"I scraped my knee." He put his arms around Logan's waist. Logan reached down and picked up Charlie in his arms. Logan tightly hugged his little boy.

"Okay. We'll go inside and get you fixed up. Where's Zoey?"

"She's in the shower."

"You did well, son. You and Gwenny make a great team." Logan took a deep breath. He was terrified at the scene he'd just witnessed. Charlie could have been badly hurt. Much to his great relief, everything had turned out well.

"Thank god," Marc nodded. He turned to Angela. "You're safe now."

Angela was struggling with her tears. "I love you," she whispered.

"*Ti amo, tesoro mio,*" Marc answered in a low voice. "I love you, my treasure."

10 A Birthday Party

Angela went back to work the next morning. When she returned to Marc's apartment that afternoon, she found him on the sofa with Gwenny curled up next to him. Her head was in his lap.

She laughed, "What are you two doing?"

"Nothing." Marc sighed and smiled. "*Il dolce far niente.*"

"English, please."

"The sweetness of doing nothing."

Angela laughed. She repeated, "*Il dolce far niente*. I'm going to remember that. I love your Italian language."

Marc moved Gwenny over. "Come and sit with me. Tell me how things went today." Angela sat and Gwenny's head rested in her lap now.

"Well, I arrived just before the clinic opened, and I found the place in an uproar. The other three veterinarians, the veterinarian assistant Lexie, and the office manager-receptionist Carol were all in the front office, and they were all talking at once. I asked them what was going on."

"What did they say?"

"Ted said they knew about Phoebe coming after me with a gun. He apologized, and he said that he and Phoebe had been having relationship problems for some time. He told her about a month ago that he wanted a divorce. He was shocked that she would go to these extremes."

"Yeah, Phoebe was furious. Off the rails," Marc added. "Oh, I forgot to mention. I talked to Detective Alvarez earlier today. Turns out that Phoebe was following Braden yesterday, apparently to see if he was doing what he was supposed to do."

"He was supposed to come after me?"

"Yes. Phoebe was almost a block behind him, tailing him, when the cops pulled him over and arrested him. That's when she came to Casa Pacifica looking for you."

"She decided to do the job herself." Angela shook her head. "I think she's a little bit nuts."

"More than a little bit. Also, about the break-in to the house where you've been staying, I bet it was Braden who did that. Phoebe may have sent him, but he's the one with the criminal record. I bet he enjoyed himself. He was trying to scare you. And those words on the wall. I bet he wrote them."

"Yes, you're probably right about that."

"So what else did you learn this morning?" Marc took her hand in his.

"Lexie and Freddy talked about the cops coming yesterday and arresting Eric. And taking vials from the meds room to test. Freddy added that they all think the cops were looking for that diluted opioid drug, hydromorphone. They are right about that. Then Carol, our office manager and receptionist, reminded us that it was time to open the clinic. She said she could see someone waiting outside with a big dog."

"Nothing about the surveillance camera and the video tape?"

"No. I guess the cops didn't tell them about that. But news about the video is going to come out in the trials."

"How do you think your co-workers will react to learning about your involvement?"

"I have no idea. Maybe they will be grateful. Maybe they will think I'm untrustworthy. I just don't know."

She leaned against Marc. "I'm trying not to worry."

He nodded and kissed her. "Yeah, worrying doesn't do any good anyway."

"I've been thinking that maybe it's time for a change." She sat up straight. "I'm thinking I might quit my job. There may be other veterinarian positions open in Tucson. Or I could start my own mobile vet service. Or I could stay at Ted's clinic, and ask for a big pay raise."

Marc smiled. "Whatever you decide to do, I'll support you. You deserve a big pay raise. You've actually helped Ted a lot."

"I hope he recognizes that." Angela frowned. "You know I already told you that Cynthia will be home this week. She and her boyfriend will be living together, so there's no more room for me. That means I have to find someplace to live. I need to find and rent an apartment."

"No, you don't."

"I don't?"

"You're moving in here with me. And Gwenny."

Gwenny raised her head and looked at Marc.

"Are you serious?" Angela asked.

"I'm dead serious."

"What do I have to do to get to live here?" She was smiling now.

"Give me Marco treats, take naked showers with me, and love me with all your heart."

"Will you let me go with you on photography expeditions?"

"I'm going on photography expeditions?"

"Yes, definitely. Will you teach me to speak Italian?"

"*Certo*."

"And do I get to do the sweetness of nothing, too?"

"*Certo. Il dolce far niente* is a skill. I'll teach you."

"Okay. It's a deal." Angela laughed.

* * *

Angela continued to go to work every day that week. She had a conference with Ted and told him about her boyfriend Marc who had installed the surveillance camera in the meds room. Later, when she returned home, she shared with Marc that she thought Ted seemed very uncomfortable when he learned about the surveillance camera. But he didn't ask her anything specific, and Angela didn't say anything revealing. She hoped that his encounters with Freddy would stay a private matter.

When she returned after work on Friday, she found Marc at the dining table. Photographs covered the table. She sat next to him.

"I've decided that I've been too hard on myself. These are not bad."

"Not bad? They are way better than not bad. I hope you see that someday soon. Meanwhile, we're going to start visiting art galleries. And the Center for Creative Photography at the University of Arizona."

Marc looked at her and smiled. "I'll go along with that."

"Hey, this one is new. I didn't know you were taking photos of Gwenny."

"She's a good model. She's beautiful, and she doesn't move much. Except when she's running, I mean."

"Yes, Gwenny is escaping the slips when she's running."

"What does that mean, 'in the slips'?"

"When I was in vet school, some of us had this game we played in which we found references to favorite animals in famous literature. The winner got a free beer. Will Shakespeare wrote a play, *Henry V*, about English King Henry V and the Battle of Agincourt. Let's see if I can remember the key part. I chose it because it mentions greyhounds. That was the point of the game, to find a favorite animal in literature."

Angela sat back and took a deep breath.

"I see you stand like greyhounds in the slips,

straining upon the start. The game's afoot;

Follow your spirit…"

"'In the slips' refers to having a slip leash around the greyhounds' necks. They are straining to escape the slips and run, run, run. There's more to that scene in the play," she added. "The rest of it is actually about troops going into battle to fight for King Henry. But I think it applies to Gwenny."

"So you're saying that Gwenny escaped the slips, and when she went to fetch the gun, she was following her spirit?"

"Yes. Exactly."

He took her hand in his and kissed it.

Gwenny on the sofa was wagging her tail now.

"Okay, Marc, it's time we get serious. Tomorrow is your birthday potluck. We're going to celebrate at your parents. I have to think of something to cook."

"No! Not a potluck! Are you crazy? My mom will cook a huge meal for us all, and she'd be offended if you bring anything to eat. Logan and Charlie and Zoey are coming from downstairs. And Li and Xochi from upstairs. We're supposed to show up between eleven and eleven thirty and eat at noon. My mom is totally thrilled that we're all coming to eat, and that she gets to cook for us."

"Fine by me. I look forward to eating your mom's cooking."

"Don't be surprised if my mom asks you a bunch of questions about you and me."

Angela grinned. "Don't worry. I have some questions for her, too."

"About what?" Marc frowned and looked at her sideways.

"About you and me." She laughed.

"Uh oh." Marc laughed, too.

* * *

Marc dressed up for his birthday party. He wore clean, almost-new jeans, a long-sleeve blue shirt, and a tie. He rolled the sleeves up at the elbow. He thought he was dressed up until he saw Angela. She had on a flowered summer dress with a tight bodice buttoned from the waist to her almost-visible cleavage, short sleeves and a mid-calf full skirt. She had several bracelets on each arm and big loop earrings. She was gorgeous, and he told her so. Angela smiled and twirled around. When she twirled, he could see above her knees. Okay. Gorgeous and sexy as hell.

The trip up into the Santa Catalina Mountains was pleasant for everyone. Logan drove his car with Zoey, Li, and Xochi as his passengers. Marc drove his car with Angela up front, and Charlie and Gwenny in the backseat.

Arrival meant that Charlie jumped out of the car with Gwenny and headed immediately for the family dogs and cats. The adults could hear him squealing and giggling as he played with the dogs who all welcomed him enthusiastically. The cats allowed Charlie to pet them, then they wandered off.

Time for lunch. Francesca brought out dish after dish and placed each one artfully on the long dining table. That included lasagna, chicken parmigiano, risotto, beef braciole, polenta, vegetables, and salad. Wine glasses were filled. Charlie got a special treat that Francesca called "*spuma*."

When Marc saw Logan frowning, he said, "Not to worry. No alcohol in *spuma*. It's mainly sparkling water, caramel, sugar and other flavors."

Logan smiled and nodded.

After the hot food was all placed on the table, Francesca said her prayer, crossed herself, then said to them all in a firm voice, "*Mangiamo!*"

Marc heard Angela whisper, "*Mangiamo.*"

They ate. And ate. And ate. Francesca was praised effusively by everyone for the delicious food. Finally, Antonio sat back and said, "*Basta.*" Enough! Marc and Angela cleared the table of dishes and brought out some small plates and forks. Francesca carried in a large homemade cake decorated with candles that were already lit.

"*Buon compleanno, mio caro figlio,*" she said, and she kissed Marc's cheek. Happy birthday, my dear son.

"*Grazie, Mamma,*" Marc said, thanking his mother. He was embarrassed and pleased at the same time.

Everyone clapped, and they sang, "Happy Birthday." Marc blew out the candles, Francesca cut the cake, and they ate. Then they all retired to the living room.

Xochi was first to speak, "Marc, I don't know you well, but I think I will soon enough. Here's my birthday gift for you. It's a handmade book with blank pages. Don't tell me it's too beautiful to write in. That will just piss me off. Use it!" She smiled.

Marc took the book, slipped the ribbon off, and looked it over. The cover was wrapped with a beautiful decorative art paper, the spine was hand-stitched, and the interior pages were a heavy writing paper. "This is very beautiful. Thank you, Xochi."

Li was next. He handed Marc a card with a calendar for the next four weeks. "I will cook one elegant Chinese meal for you each week for the next month. We'll have to plan ahead the day and time of day for the meal to accommodate our schedules. You fill in the days on the calendar. Happy birthday, Marc. I'm glad you're home."

"Oh, Li! I love your cooking. Thanks! And I'm glad to be home, too."

Zoey spoke next. "Logan and I bought season tickets for you and a guest to attend the Arizona basketball games that start in the fall. Don't let Charlie talk you into being your guest for every game. Angela should get to go with you."

"That's totally cool. Thank you. I love basketball."

Charlie handed Marc a drawing he'd done of Gwenny. "Happy Birthday, Marc."

"Dude! What a great drawing! Thanks!"

Charlie giggled and went to sit with Gwenny.

Logan said, "I have a little extra. Here's a hardcover copy of my first book, just published. The title is *Social Philosophy in the 21st Century*."

"Wow. I'm impressed. I'll definitely read it." Marc took the book and opened it. "And you signed it. Thanks, Logan."

"I have some good news, too," Logan added. "I've been hired to teach philosophy classes at Pima Community College as an adjunct professor. I'll keep my job as our apartment manager, too, which means lower rent. We won't be rich, but, at least, we don't have to leave Tucson to find a job."

"Great news, Logan."

"Your mamma and I have something for you, too," Marc's dad Antonio said. "We're funding an all expenses-paid round trip to someplace nice to visit. Choose a place with art, music, and good food. I suggest New Orleans."

Marc looked over at Angela. She laughed and shrugged her shoulders. He knew then that they would be going to New Orleans, maybe for Mardi Gras. He looked back at his dad. "Thanks so much. It will be great to travel to a place with no bombs going off."

Angela handed Marc a card. Inside he found a document indicating that he was now an official member of the Center for Creative Photography at the University of Arizona. He nodded shyly, and said, "Perfect. Thank you, Angela." He passed the card around for everyone to see.

"I have a little something extra, too. I'll tell you later," she said.

Marc wiggled his eyebrows and grinned.

Later, following an afternoon spent talking and laughing, they said their goodbyes. Logan, Zoey, Li, and Xochi left first, followed closely by Marc and Angela. Both Charlie and Gwenny fell asleep almost immediately in the backseat of Marc's car.

"So what's this other extra gift you have for me? Lots of Marco treats?"

"That goes without saying. You are irresistible, you know."

"That's good to hear."

"No, this is something a little more serious. Did you know that you talk in your sleep?"

"I do?" Marc frowned. "What do I say?"

"You cry out, 'No! No!'" Angela's smile was sad. "You're having nightmares. I think you have PTSD from your wartime experiences. So I called Cass. He's back on their horse farm near Whiteriver. Cass told me about their equine therapy sessions. He's an Army vet, and he told me that he was badly hurt in Afghanistan. He came home severely injured, and he's suffered from occasional bouts of PTSD. He thinks that's what you've been going through. Cass thinks, and I agree, that you will benefit from one of their equine therapy sessions with other vets."

"But I'm not a vet."

"Cass says if you were in the middle of warfare, if you saw death and destruction, if you were being shot at, if you are suffering from a weariness of spirit, then you qualify, even though you were a journalist, not a soldier. He told me to tell you that he would be very honored if you joined him in one of their sessions. He thinks you can contribute as well as benefit. He has a horse picked out just for you."

"Wow." Marc fell silent for long minutes. Finally he spoke. "He's right. You're right. Okay. I'll accept your birthday gift to me, Angela. Thank you."

Angela had tears in her eyes now.

"Why are you crying?" Marc was confused.

"You go up there for one of those equine therapy sessions for a whole week, and I will miss you!"

Marc laughed. "I love you."

"And I love you."

"Can I have a Marco treat when we get home?"

"Of course."

He was quiet again, and then he said, "I think I'm in the slips now."

"Yes, dear Marco. Follow your spirit. Follow your spirit."

Thank you and some Information Sources:

Hello Reader!

Thank you for reading *In the Slips*, the third Iron Horse Mystery. Please leave a review of this book wherever you buy books (Amazon, Kobo, Nook, Apple, etc.) and also at Bookbub and Goodreads. By leaving a review for others to read, you can make it much easier for mystery readers everywhere to find this book. Thank you so much. Please sign up for my monthly newsletter all about art, books, and the natural world at www.cjshane.com/contactnewsletter.html

Here are some sources for more information:

To learn more about the work photojournalists in war zones, read this excellent article in the *Guardian* by Corinne Dufka. https://www.theguardian.com/artanddesign/2023/sep/26/corinne-dufka-war-photographer-book

Look for more about animal psychology and behavior, go to American College of Veterinary Behavior. https://www.dacvb.org/

And if you want to speak Italian with hand gestures, check out this amusing video, *How to Talk with Your Hands: Italian Hand Gestures*, from a different Marco (a real person), Marco Danesi.

https://www.youtube.com/watch?v=_8hAOxsTpVY

A key to Italian pronunciation. "ch" is a "k" sound – chianti wine; "ci" is a "ch" sound – "ciao"

Racing Greyhounds

Greyhounds are raced on tracks in a number of countries around the world, especially in Australia, Ireland, the United Kingdom and the United States. Racing was more prevalent in the U.S. in the past, but, over time, tracks have been closed down in most states. Currently the states where greyhound racing is legal are Alabama, Arkansas, Iowa, Texas and West Virginia, but the only active racing tracks are in West Virginia. Needless to say, legalized gambling and racing go hand-and-hand. Greyhound racing and horse racing are comparable.

These beautiful dogs don't have the best life when they are kept for racing. Usually they stay in enclosures until it's time to go out to the track and race. Deep connections with humans are rarely an option. In addition, most greyhounds are retired after four to six years as racers. What happens to them then? If they have been fast on the track, they may be kept to breed the next generation of racers.

Greyhounds have a reputation of being easy-going. In fact, the term most used to describe them is "couch potatoes." They usually get along well with other pets and children, and they don't typically bark a lot. They do like to run so they shouldn't be left off leash in case they spot something to chase, like a cat or another dog. They need to run because it's their thing so take them to the dog park or a place safe from vehicles so they can get their exercise.

And like Gwenny in this story, these retired racers don't have a lot of experience with going up and down stairs.

Volunteers have stepped forward around the U.S. to find forever homes for the retired racers. Because of the popularity of racing in other countries, some retired racers are being brought to the U.S. from countries such as Australia and Ireland.

A few years ago, I decided to adopt a retired greyhound. In the past, I had lived with two whippets so I decided it was time for a greyhound. Both whippets and greyhounds are sight hounds. I went to Southern Arizona Greyhound Rescue and was directed to a foster home that was taking care of four dogs. To my surprise, the dog that caught my attention was a mix, a greyhound-border collie who had been found half-starved on the streets of Yuma, Arizona. That's how he got his name – Yuma. I couldn't resist him. Yuma jumped in the backseat of the car right away, and he came home with me. He was border collie-smart and greyhound-couch potato lazy. He quickly decided that I was his responsibility so if any other person or animal approached me, he would move in front of me with that border collie warning look on his face directed at the person or dog approaching. Once, he gave a Border Patrol agent "the look." The agent grinned and backed away. "I don't want your dog to eat me," he laughed.

To find if your state has a volunteer adoption option for greyhounds, go to:
https://www.grey2kusa.org/action/adopt.php

And here are videos from individuals who adopted retired racing greyhounds.

Video of an Australian racer adopted into an Australian family.

The beach is a great place to run.

https://www.youtube.com/watch?v=iVJyVQ4uT8s
Video of a rescue greyhound in an American family.
Oh those stairs! So scary! Another rescue challenged by stairs.
https://www.youtube.com/watch?v=DEtyL4lXp7s
Reasons to get a greyhound:
Watch greyhounds sleeping on the couch and running zoomies
https://www.youtube.com/watch?v=58ZOTTEK300

Iron Horse Next in Series? Clouds

1. Sunday Potluck

David Li Liang checked the boiling pot on his stove then glanced at the stove's clock. Three more minutes. He sighed and went to sit on his sofa. Bonita, the almost-grown kitten, or maybe she should be called a cat now, came to sit on his lap. He began to stroke her, and Bonita purred contentedly.

"You're kinda spoiled, you know?" Li said. Bonita looked up at him with her big golden eyes and purred even louder. She was a tri-color calico cat, which, for Li, was the prettiest kitty in the world.

He sighed again. "Dumplings. I'm taking dumplings to the potluck again." That's what his fellow residents at Casa Pacifica Apartments called his *jiaozi* at their Sunday potluck dinners. Or worse, Italian "*ravioli*." He grimaced. As if the English or Italians were the first at making those delicious meat and veggie-filled, small dough bundles with their edges pressed together, and then boiled in hot water. Ridiculous! The Italians got their dumplings from China! The story was that Marco Polo brought *jiaozi* back to Italy when he returned from his travels. *Jiaozi*'s origin was China!

"So why can't they use the proper name?" he groused. Bonita purred even louder.

Li frowned. On top of that, his *jiaozi* had some excellent *jiangyou* sauce poured over them, too, sauce that came all the way from Zhejiang Province in China. Just as *jiaozi* became "dumplings" at the Sunday potlucks, the potluck gang transformed *jiangyou* into "soy sauce." Li just couldn't get it. Mandarin Chinese words were not *that* hard to say. They had no trouble saying Spanish or French words, but they wouldn't even try Mandarin.

Charlie was the exception. Logan Reid, Casa Pacifica's manager, had a five-year-old son named Charlie, and Charlie seemed to be the only one with an adventuresome spirit when it came to trying new words. Li had already taught Charlie how to say a couple of Mandarin phrases. He laughed to himself. Maybe he'd teach Charlie even more Mandarin, the two of them would have their own conversations, and the adults wouldn't understand a word.

Meanwhile, he had to make *jiaozi* way too often, always at their request. He was one of Tucson's top chefs, he knew how to make a long list of delicious Chinese dishes, but no. It had to be *jiaozi*. If they started pouring Italian or Mexican sauces on his *jiaozi*, he was going to quit, and start making tacos every Sunday! It would serve them right. He shook his head.

"Truth be told, I'm not really mad about the *jiaozi*," he muttered to Bonita. He knew what was making him so annoyed. It was his parents who were bothering the hell out of him. His parents and their "suggestion" that he get married, and worse, get married to a girl they had picked out for him. No way! *That* was what was bothering him. And if he admitted it to himself, he was getting a little tired of his chef job. His restaurant manager was a worry wart, stressed out all the time, and now the manager was putting pressure on everyone in the kitchen to work harder faster. Why not just chill out? On top of all that, Laurel was gone now so he didn't even have the relief of physical pleasure with her.

"Bonita, I'm very cranky. I need to get over myself before I go join the others." He looked at the clock. Time was up for the damn dumplings.

He pushed Bonita onto the sofa, went to the stove, turned it off, and drained the pot of all the hot water. Then he transferred the *jiaozi* to a large ceramic serving bowl. He added the *jiangyou* sauce.

Li carefully placed the very full and very hot ceramic bowl into his favorite carrying basket. Yes, the bowl was hot from freshly cooked *jiaozi*, but he was going immediately to Logan's apartment downstairs for the regular Sunday potluck. He would be able to get the bowl out of the basket and on a table trivet pretty quickly without burning himself or the basket.

Li glanced in the mirror on his way out. He didn't look too bad. His goatee and mustache were neatly trimmed, his long dark hair was tied back into a braid, and he was wearing a new shirt, sort of a pale blue color. He never wore white when he wasn't working. White was too much like the uniform he wore as a chef. Li closed his door behind him, making sure that Bonita the cat stayed inside his apartment and didn't go wandering. This was the time of evening that the coyotes came out, and they were looking for something good to eat, preferably a chubby little kitty.

Thinking about the potluck made Li wonder who would be there tonight. Okay, so apartment manager Logan and his boy Charlie would definitely be there, and Logan's girlfriend, Zoey, the biology teacher who lived downstairs in her own apartment. Marc and Angela would probably be there, too. Angela had just moved in with Marc, and they seemed very happy together. The two of them had a big dog named Gwenny. Bonita had not met Gwenny yet. Probably for the best. Gwenny seemed pretty tame, but she was a big dog, a greyhound. Bonita would be terrified.

Li's thoughts turned to the newest resident in their Casa Pacifica apartment building in the Iron Horse district of Tucson. Xochi. He'd first met her when she and Angela were assaulted by some dipwad who vandalized Angela's mobile veterinarian van, whacked both women in their faces, and then ran away. Her name was Xochi, obviously a Mexican name. Sounded like "SO-chee." She was very pretty, with a sort of feisty manner and a "don't mess with me" attitude. Her apartment was upstairs, too, down the hall from him, but he hadn't seen much of her, despite being really curious about her. He knew she was some kind of artist. She made artist's books, whatever that was. He thought artists painted or made sculptures, not books. Yes, he looked forward to knowing her better.

He knocked on Logan's door and then opened it.

"Hey, Li. Come on in," Logan called out. He was wearing a chef's apron and holding a large spoon in his hand. "I've made a veggie-chicken stew. It's almost ready."

Li approached the long dining table, pulled the ceramic bowl out of his basket and put it on a trivet. Li respected Logan a lot, and trusted him, too. Li had found Logan to be a fair and capable manager of the apartment building where they lived, and over time, he'd come to admire Logan, too. The man was a real intellectual who was finishing his doctoral degree in philosophy, of all things. Li could have been intimated because he didn't know beans about philosophy. But Logan was never arrogant, and Li had come to admire what a good job Logan did of fathering Charlie. He thought of Logan as a real friend.

"I brought some…," Li hesitated. "...dumplings." He looked into the living area and saw Marc, Angela, and the new resident, Xochi, sitting together. He waved, and they all said hello and waved back.

Just then, Charlie came running out of his bedroom with Gwenny the greyhound on his heels. "Dumplings!" he said in a loud voice. He stopped suddenly, and Gwenny ran into his backside. Charlie laughed loudly as the dog skidded into him. "No! I mean *jiaozi!*"

Li chuckled. "That's right. So Charlie, '*Ni jiào shénme míngzì?*'" What's your name?

Charlie giggled and started jumping up and down. '*Wo jiào cháli.*'" My name is Charlie.

"Very good." Li was grinning now. They'd practiced this earlier. Now it was time to try something new. He pointed at Gwenny and asked, "'*Tā jiào shénme míngzì?*'" What's her name?

For a moment, Charlie looked blank, then he asked, "'*Tā*'?"

Li nodded. He put his hand on his chest and said, "*Wo,*" then pointed at Charlie and said, "*Ni,*" then pointed at Gwenny. "*Tā. Tā jiào shénme míngzì?*"

Charlie nodded and giggled, "*Tā jiào Gwenny.*" Her name is Gwenny.

"*Hao de, hao de.*" Very good. Li was grinning now. "Your colloquial Mandarin is very good."

"What's 'colloquial?'" Charlie looked confused.

"Common language. Words used most often."

Charlie turned and threw his arms around the greyhound who was wagging her tail. "I love you, Gwenny."

"*Wo ài ni.* That means 'I love you.'" Li said.

"*Wo ài ni,* Gwenny!" Charlie couldn't stop giggling. Gwenny's tail wagged faster.

Li glanced around. All the adults were grinning, too. Xochi smiled at him and said, "Impressive. You're a good language teacher."

Li suddenly felt embarrassed. He was acting like a show off. First cranky, and then a show off. What the hell is wrong with me? he asked himself. He looked up and saw both Logan and his girlfriend Zoey grinning proudly.

"I didn't know that you are teaching him Chinese," Zoey said.

"Yeah, Mandarin. Charlie is really sharp. He likes to learn new things."

Logan nodded. "Yes, I'm really proud of him." He stepped away from the table. "Charlie, go wash your hands and be quick about it. It's time to eat. Everyone come and have a seat at the table."

A few minutes later, they were all seated together for their Sunday potluck.

"Thank you all for coming," Logan said. "I made this stew, and Zoey grilled some salmon steaks."

"I made a creole rice and beans dish. It includes some smoked sausage," Angela added. "My mom used to make it, New Orleans style."

"I made nothing. I'm lazy," Marc added. Everyone chuckled.

"And I made dumplings again," Li shrugged his shoulders.

"Good thing. We'd have to protest if we don't get our dumplings," Logan nodded.

"*Jiaozi*, Daddy," Charlie said.

"Okay. *Jiaozi*," Logan replied.

Li smiled and nodded. Maybe Charlie would take care of the language problem for him.

Logan poured wine, passed the glasses around, and handed Charlie a glass of orange juice. They commenced eating. The meal went fast and, not long after, they were seated in a circle in Logan's living room.

"I'd like to know what everyone has been up to," Logan said. "I'll start. I'll begin teaching my Introduction to Philosophy class at Pima Community College this week. I'll have a second class in Social Philosophy the next day. And I'm working on an academic paper about human rights, specifically the right to privacy versus freedom of expression in the context of digital media."

"Wow! That's a mouthful," Marc said. Marc Tomassone had returned to Tucson only recently after long months away working as a photojournalist in war zones. He brought Gwenny the greyhound with him, very quickly met veterinarian Dr. Angela Brooks, they fell in love, and not long after, Angela became part of the Casa Pacifica family. Gwenny spent part of her time with Marc and Angela, and a good bit of time as well with Charlie. Gwenny and Charlie adored each other.

"Yeah," Logan chuckled. "Most people aren't interested in what I do unless it affects them directly. Then they suddenly discover that they have an opinion on the subject. In this case, folks seem to be interested in the topic." He took Zoey's hand in his. "Tell us what you're up to."

"Spring semester is finished. I'm going to teach a summer biology course at the high school, and I'm thinking about applying for a grant to start an ornithology program for five- and six-year-olds. We'll go birding a couple of times a week, always early in the day before it gets too hot."

"I'm going with her if that happens!" Charlie said enthusiastically. "And right now, I'm going to summer camp every day."

Logan shifted attention to Marc. "How about you?"

"Angela convinced me that I'm not half bad at photography. I mean art photography. So I've been wandering around Tucson and taking photos. I'm starting to enter my work into some local art exhibits." Angela took his hand and smiled. Marc added, "This is way more fun than taking photos of people shooting each other in war zones." He nodded to Angela.

"My boss gave me a pay raise at my job," Angela grinned. "And I'm spending more time in the clinic and less time in the mobile vet unit. My boss is definitely hiring two new vet assistants, and he may even hire a new veterinarian who will take over the mobile unit. We're really busy."

"Li? How's your chef job? And how's your friend Laurel?"

"Laurel and I parted company," Li said. "She was accepted into Princeton University's law school so she's moved back east to New Jersey. I could have gone with her, but I don't think I would be happy there. It's okay. She's doing what she wants, and so am I. We parted on good terms. No hard feelings." He shrugged his shoulders. "Not much else is new." He looked at Xochi. "Tell us about you." He didn't want to talk about any of the cranky stuff.

"Everything is going well. I turned my second bedroom into a studio, and I've already taught two book arts classes there. Photos of one of my artist's books will be included in an art book to be published soon. The book is devoted exclusively to artist's books so it's a real honor for me to be included. And…"

Suddenly there was a crashing sound that came from above them, then some thumping sounds.

Xochi jumped up. "That noise came from my apartment!" She moved quickly toward the door. "Someone is in my apartment!"

Li immediately followed her. "I'll go with you. If there's an intruder, he may try to confront you."

Logan and Marc were on their feet now, too. Logan turned to Charlie, "You stay here with Zoey."

Just as Xochi opened Logan's door, they all could hear the sound of someone running down the upstairs hallway in their apartment building. As they stepped into the hall, a form dressed in dark clothing and a black mask could be seen rushing down the stairs and exiting the building through the small laundry room and backdoor.

"I'll follow him!" Logan said. "He may go out back down the alley."

Marc was opening the front door at the same time. "I'll go out front in case he comes around and tries to run down the street."

By now, Xochi and Li were already upstairs at Xochi's apartment, which was directly above Logan's. Xochi reached out for the closed door, which opened easily. "Look! Someone must have picked the lock."

Li stepped forward. "Let me go in first. There may still be someone here." He entered the apartment ahead of her. He could feel Xochi close to him, her hand on his back. The apartment was silent.

Xochi moved forward and looked around Li. "I don't see anything disturbed. I'll look in my bedroom and studio." Li followed her. She glanced around the living room, then she went to her bedroom. "Looks okay," she said. Then she went to the extra bedroom that she had transformed into a studio and a room for small classes. Li came to her side. Xochi gasped.

The room was trashed. The only piece of furniture that had not been overturned was the large, heavy table in the middle of the room. There were three six- and eight-foot tall shelving units that had been overturned. Art supplies were everywhere. Li could see large cardboard folders full of art papers of various weights that were scattered across the floor. Also on the floor were jars of stencil paints and bottles of various colored inks, tubes of acrylic paint, and a couple of large plastic gallon containers full of some thick white liquid. The lid of one of the gallon containers had come off, and the white liquid had spilled onto numerous items.

Xochi reached over and sat the plastic gallon container upright. "Oh, god. What a mess! There's PVA glue all over the place. And my container of methyl cellulose powder is dumped out, too." She turned and opened the door to the room's closet. Same thing. The shelves were empty, and what had been on the shelves was now on the floor.

Li looked down at Xochi. He could see the tears in her eyes as she looked up at him.

"I don't understand. Who would do something like this? There's so much damage. It's going to cost me a lot to replace everything. And a lot of time to clean up this mess."

He put his arm around her shoulders. "I'll help you. What about your work? Your artist's books, I mean?"

"They're in containers in drawers in that big chest in the living room." She walked back into the living room. "Nothing disturbed there."

Logan and Marc appeared. Logan was shaking his head. "He got away. I didn't see him at all in the back."

"And he wasn't in the front either. I'm going to check the video surveillance camera we set up earlier," Marc added.

"Xochi, what about the lock on your door?" Logan asked.

Xochi took a look. "It must have been picked. I don't see any damage or signs that the door was forced."

"No one has a copy of your key?" Marc asked

"No." Xochi shook her head.

"What about previous tenants?" he asked Logan.

"I have the locks to individual apartments changed every time there's a change of residents. So it can't be that," Logan said. "Let's go down to my apartment. We can call the cops, and I want to check the front and back doors."

Ten minutes later they were all back in Logan's apartment. He looked and found that either the front door or the back door of the apartment building had been picked open. He decided it was the back door. No damage had been done, but the back door was unlocked. By that time, Marc had retrieved the video from the surveillance camera.

Marc gestured to the screen. "Here he is at the back door. He appears to be a man from his build, and he's fairly tall. He's dressed all in black. You can see him pull a tool out from his back pocket and start messing with the back door lock. It only takes him a minute to get the door open."

Logan shook his head. "I'll have to talk to the owners and get better locks."

There was a knock at Logan's door, and when he opened it, two Tucson police officers in uniform were standing there.

Logan introduced himself, explained the situation, and led them upstairs to Xochi's apartment. They all stood aside as she opened her door. The cops went in, examined the debris, took photos and notes, and asked a few questions. Logan noticed that they also dusted for fingerprints. They took Xochi's fingerprints, too, so they would know hers as well.

One of the cops with the name tag "Officer Morales" on his chest said, "Okay. We have the basic information and photos. One of our detectives will be around in the morning to ask more questions. Meanwhile, Ms. Navarro, I suggest you compile a list of missing and damaged or destroyed items. And since your building's outer doors and your apartment door are so easy to break into, perhaps you could spend the night in a safer place. The perpetrator might return."

Li frowned. He didn't like this at all. Neither did Logan or Marc who were both frowning, too.

The police officers left, and Logan turned to Xochi. "Do you have somewhere you can go?"

Xochi shook her head. "No, it's too late now to call any friends. I don't have any family here in Tucson." She shrugged her shoulders. "I'll just stay in my apartment. Whoever did this made a huge mess and caused a lot of damage. I seriously doubt that they will return."

The three men, Zoey, and Angela all shook their heads.

"How about if you sleep on our couch?" Logan asked her.

"Oh, I think you are all making too big a deal of this."

"Please reconsider, Xochi," Zoey said.

"Okay. That's it. I'm sleeping on your couch, or you're sleeping on my couch," Li said firmly.

Everyone nodded their approval. Everyone but Xochi. She giggled.

"What's so funny?" Li frowned. "Think I can't take care of you? I know a little *gong fu*."

"I don't know what's funny," she answered. Then Xochi burst into tears.

Zoey and Angela put their arms around her as she sobbed. "Listen to Li," Angela said. "He's trying to help you. He knows *gong fu*." She turned to Li and whispered, "What's *gong f u*?"

"Chinese martial arts," Li answered. "*Kung fu*, if you prefer." He was annoyed. Does Xochi think just because he's a chef, he doesn't know how to take care of a woman?

Xochi wiped away her tears and looked up at Li. "Thank you for the offer. May I please sleep on your couch tonight?"

"Yes, you may," he answered in a serious tone of voice. "Bring your favorite pillow." Li felt a sudden sense of elation. He wasn't sure why.

Logan spoke up. "Okay, it's getting late. It's way past Charlie's bedtime. Let's all settle down for the night. Li, I'll text you in the morning when the detective arrives, no doubt with a long list of questions. We'll get the investigation going. We need to find out who did this and why, so it doesn't happen again. Meanwhile, I'm going to start work on getting better locks for all our doors."

Li and Xochi headed upstairs to fetch her pillow, and then they went directly to his apartment.

2 Clouds

Logan Reid was in the kitchen making coffee when he heard Zoey tiptoe across his living room. She was coming from his bedroom to open his front door so she could return to her apartment before Charlie woke up. He turned and smiled at her. "Come back for breakfast," he whispered. Zoey grinned and nodded.

They had made this arrangement when they'd become lovers, and they'd been following it for a while. He'd given her the key to his place, and, almost every night, Zoey left her apartment and crept into his. The purpose of all the secrecy was to keep life as usual for Charlie. Logan didn't want to have to explain what he and Zoey did in bed together, which was so much more than sleep. Charlie was too young. So he'd suggested the arrangement, and Zoey agreed. Truth be told, Logan found it very exciting. This sweet, beautiful woman sneaking into his apartment and into his bed was the best thing ever.

Logan heard his cell phone beep. He took a quick look and saw a text from Detective Alvarez informing him that he would arrive by nine a.m. Logan responded affirmatively, then texted Li to tell him of the detective's arrival. He texted Marc, too. Time to wake up Charlie.

Half an hour later, Charlie and Zoey were sitting with Logan at his dining table, all three eating breakfast and discussing the day's plans.

"I'm going to a faculty meeting at the high school this morning," Zoey said.

"I'm going to summer camp today," Charlie grinned. "I like summer camp."

"I know you're going to be busy, Logan, so I'll take Charlie to catch the bus so he can make it to camp on time," Zoey added. "Then I'll go on to my meeting."

"Thanks, Zoey. I think the meeting with Detective Alvarez may go on a while. This is a rather strange and complicated situation. Xochi hasn't lived here very long, yet the break-in seems directed only at her. None of the other residents' apartments were affected, just Xochi's, and only one room in her apartment was trashed, not the entire place. This brings up a lot of questions." Logan turned to Charlie. "Looks like you're finished eating. Go brush your teeth. It's almost time to go."

"I'm going to go brush my teeth, too, Mr. Logan. Someone may want to kiss me."

Logan grabbed her and kissed her hard on her lips. "Come back, soon, Zoey Corban."

Only a few minutes later, Zoey and Charlie were gone, and Logan was cleaning up after breakfast.

* * *

Li woke up early. He stretched and took a deep breath. Bonita was on the pillow next to him, purring as usual. What to do today? Oh, yeah. His morning tai ji class had been canceled. Suddenly, he sat up in bed, eyes wide open. There was a beautiful woman sleeping on his couch! How could he forget that? *She* is what he would be doing today. Li thought he might just call in to work and tell them that he was sick or bored with his job or something. He didn't want to leave her. He wanted to stay and help Xochi.

He looked over at his clock, then pulled himself out of bed and headed to the bathroom. He quietly tiptoed into his kitchen after taking a peek at Xochi on his couch. She was snuggled in the blanket he'd given her last night, curly, long dark hair tousled against her pillow. She appeared to be sound asleep. So he went to the kitchen and made a pot of coffee. Maybe the scent of hot coffee would wake her up.

No. Still sound asleep. He sipped the coffee. She needed to wake up because that cop Logan told them about would show up this morning. How could he wake her up in a gentle way? Suddenly he thought of his guitar. Yes, some sweet, soft music on his acoustic guitar was called for. Maybe that would work. Li put down his cup, found his guitar, and sat down on a chair, not too close and not too far, from Xochi. He began playing one of his favorite tunes.

Xochi stirred, turned over, sat up, and yawned. She focused on Li, and watched him play. She sat quietly, concentrating on the music and on his fingers moving on the strings.

When Li finished the tune, he looked at her and smiled, "Want some coffee?"

"Sure. But more than that, I want to know what you were playing. Tell me about that tune. I love it."

"The tune is called '*Nuages*.' It's pretty old, written in 1939 or 1940 by a French Romani jazz guitarist named Django Reinhardt. Apparently he wrote it to express sadness at the Nazi occupation of Paris, and also to express sadness at the loss of a lover. It's an example of what's called "gypsy swing" music."

"That word, '*nuages*.' It's French?"

"Yes, it means 'clouds.' The lyrics are about how the clouds can darken the light of sun, and how the singer's heart could become dark, too, if he ever lost his lover."...